Then The Trees Said Hello

HJ CORNING

HAPPY CAMPRR PRESS

Lying in the midday sun
Not knowing my real life had just begun
Lying under the tree's safe arms, I know I can feel no harm.

You probably won't believe what I'm about to tell you. I wouldn't. You shouldn't have to believe it. But here it is, The Truth. I wrote this all down in a journal, hoping someone would find it someday, long after I was gone. If I told this story myself, the consequences would be too great. I just want people to know what's real.

—Sara

Prologue

I keep thinking of that day at the pond and wondering if I'd been better off just staying there. If I'd never noticed that bright spot at the bottom of the pond- or just left it alone?

My life would be so different. I wouldn't be constantly on the run. In perpetual walk mode. I wouldn't always be looking at every person I meet as if they might hurt me or the things I love.

And then again, that emptiness would persist. The sense that I hadn't really accomplished much in my life. Worse, that I wasn't caring for the gifts I'd been given.

Now I know I've made a difference. Now I know that I've helped. And even if they do find me, I'll have influenced my part of the world. Creating an effect that will be felt for centuries to come.

Sara

Tuesday morning was lightly foggy, but I could already feel the heat rising from the road as Bessie, Clem, and I drove to Don's office on the other side of town. Clem was sniffing the air expectantly, like he knew something was about to happen.

It was while I was out on one of my trips five years earlier that I'd found my dog, Clem. He was just a little ball of fur on his own in the woods. I don't know how he survived. The coyotes must've thought he looked too strange to mess with him.

The drool never stopped oozing from his mouth. One of his gums hung lower than the other, and the tops of his ears had been scorched off. I didn't even want to think how. But here he was on his own, only a few months old. I gave him some of my jerky and water, and by my feet he stayed from then on.

Clem grew up to be an Akita, big and strong. His only strangeness was that he was afraid of the sound of plastic bags, and every once in a while he just shook, like he was having his own personal earthquake. He'd slump to the ground, and in seconds he'd pop back up, like nothing had happened at all and return to whatever he was doing. He'd helped keep me warm on cold nights, and he'd licked away a lot of tears.

***

The bluish paint on the siding where Don's office was, desperately needed attention. Years of putting money into the business, and not the space, gave it a feeling of neglect. It was obvious that the moss-covered roof would need to be fixed sooner rather than later. Low key, and low maintenance, the nondescript building reminded me of Don himself.

In the door window, I caught a glimpse of the ends of my knife-cut hair hanging below my baseball cap. It had lightened up quite a bit in the last few weeks since I'd last seen a mirror. Luckily, I no longer cared that I looked like a struggling maple tree during a summer storm.

Don had called me into his office the moment I got back to town. He didn't waste time with pleasantries. "Sara, we're gonna have to let you go."

I sat with my mouth agape, not knowing whether to cry or celebrate. I'd been waiting for this day, but I wasn't prepared-so all I could do was sit and stare. I knew it was coming. I just didn't want to see it.

They hadn't been happy with my work for quite some time. I was saving too many trees, he said.

How is it possible that's even a thing? But there it was. They weren't in the tree saving business. They were in the tree harvesting business. Without which houses couldn't be built, paper couldn't be made. "For God's sake, Sara, where do ya' think toilet paper comes from?"

Like that was going to change my mind.

I spent weeks on end in the woods all around Washington marking plots of trees ready to be cut.

The Olympic Peninsula was my favorite area to work. The Sitka spruce, straight and strong and a ready harbor from any storm. The enveloping red alders, creating tunnels, like marriage bowers. Keeping the piercing sun off my skin, their trunks were eloquently curved, as if they were always dancing in the wind. The subtle green moss covered their bark, providing a blanket of nourishment and wetness. On the Olympic Peninsula, the moisture dripped from the atmosphere; you could just lick the air and quench your thirst.

Many of the red alders shot straight up and created an overlapping series of umbrellas, but some of them took another path. Their branches reached up and down and to the ground, with bobbles and lumps and bumps. Like people who color their hair, these were the artists of the alder world, creating their own path, providing nooks and crannies for nests and resting places for their animal friends.

***

I'd felt like an empty pail for the last few months, just trying to keep everyone happy and stay in the box of how work and my family expected me to act. They really just wanted me to go back and be the mute Sara who kept to herself. I wished I could sometimes. My head was a swirl and my brain was buzzing.

This is one reason I love being in the woods, far from the expectations of people. Among their thoughts and emotions, I lost track of my own. In the woods I fit in and felt safe. As much as the Riley community was my family, I still felt like the adopted alien. The tension between my brother, Brian, and I had escalated to heights I didn't know existed. Mom was caught in the middle, so she did nothing

Once I started hearing them, it was increasingly hard to do my job, but I didn't know how to quit. Guess I didn't have to. I wanted to protect the trees. They'd become my best friend and wise council. I marked fewer and fewer for cutting but I knew I really wasn't protecting them, I at least felt like I was doing something. It was better than doing nothing.

Before I heard the trees, I worked in a sort of quiet contemplation. It was just Clem and I walking in the woods for days at a time. Clem was a great help in my marking off for tree cuttings. I taught him to carry the line and where to stop. It really reduced the number of steps I took, and it really increased the amount of food I carried. He carried his own, of course, but he always wanted some of mine. My fault, I guess, for giving him that jerky the first day.

Now I feared I'd never get back to that place of quiet I had before they opened me up to a whole new world. These days It seemed like a distant cousin I'd met when I was five. I had a faint recollection of our time together but couldn't remember if we had anything in common.

I needed more time. I thought I did anyway. Now I needed to grow up and hit life head on, let the things that had transpired trickle down into my bones and fibers- trust my gut and move from there. You know, how when you look back and find something was perfect? It was unexpected, but perfect? I'd spent my twenties, working for Ditton's in the woods on my own. They paid for my college. My entire world was just sitting there waiting for me to arrive after I graduated. I thought I was the luckiest person alive! Then they told me my job was to spend a week in the woods surveying the trees.

"What's the catch?".

Don had told me, "No catch. You'll just be out in the woods by yourself for a week with no way of talking to anybody."

"And why doesn't anyone else want this job?"

"Because they don't want to leave their families." He responded matter-of-factly.

I beamed. "When do I start?!"

I couldn't believe I got to sleep outside for weeks and they paid me well! I had nothing to spend my money on, so it just accumulated. Mom said she was investing it. I didn't know what that meant and didn't really care. I had everything I needed. I worked in the place where I would vacation. When I wasn't in the woods, I was at Mom's.

So even though the way I understood trees and animals had completely changed, I couldn't bring myself to quit. I couldn't imagine what else I'd do. The trees had become something so much more than a job, or things I studied, but I really didn't know how to explain that to anybody then.

"We're really sorry, Sara," Don's limp cheeks, and compassionate eyes hadn't changed since I was a kid. It was almost like I could remember looking into them at my baptism. He'd been my kind Dad, since my biological Dad couldn't be. "We think of you as family, but we're a business and we have workers and shareholders to support- and that equals trees. Here's a check for the six months of vacation you've banked. I wish I could pay out your sick time. You never missed a day."

I looked at Don's chin as words poured out of his mouth.

Don looked away. "Sara, I'm sorry. I wish I didn't have to do this; I feel like I'm firing a daughter. I don't know what you're gonna do. Don't know if anyone in the loggin' industry will have you. I wish you'd change your mind about all this." His voice was filled with regret.

How could I just change my mind about something that was so real? I just wanted people to know what I knew without thinking I was nuts.

That was long ago. And it's where this story began.

Maxine

I should've picked a better date to meet Detroit, my dad.

"Well, look at you. You, an adult and all! Looks like your mom did a mighty fine job of raising ya." We were sitting at a little local restaurant. Detroit had suggested we meet here when I told him over the phone, I was coming to meet him.

"Yes, she did." I responded, surprised by his demeanor. *Was this why Mom tried to keep me from meeting my dad?*

There was the ordering of coffee and pancakes in between these words. Not interesting enough to go into. Due to his name, it hadn't been much of a challenge to find my biological Father even though Mom would only tell me he was in Texas. Their relationship was an eighteen-year old's mistake she'd said, "except that I got you." Was always her reply when I asked about my dad.

Detroit asked when the air between us became silent. "So tell me about all the boys you've been datin'." "I date girls, not boys." I lowered my eyes. I didn't know how he'd respond. And it was weird to think my dad didn't know this important detail about me.

His full cup of hot coffee crashed down on the table, splashed and scalded my hands filled with a pancaked fork.

"You kiddin'? MY kid, a kid with MY genes, is a queer! Your mom should've let me raise ya'. I wouldn't have raised no sissy!" He was yelling like he wanted the whole town to hear. I put my trembling fork down and put my hand on my forehead. I raised my eyes looking for an exit, but the whole restaurant was staring at us. Now everyone there knew I was gay, and in this area, I wasn't sure that was a good thing.

The server rushed over, her cowboy boots pounding her arrival. "What's gotten into you Detroit? You better leave me a big tip for havin' to clean up your mess." Her brown plastic name tag crookedly pressed against the chest of her plaid shirt.

Dad pinched her on the butt of her strained Levi's. She squealed and laughed. "Watch where you put those hands. I'll have Buster after you!" said her mouth, but the rest of her face seemed to enjoy the attention.

"I ain't scared of that ole' wussie man of yours," replied Detroit with a big grin on his face. "You come over anytime and I'll show you what it means to be a man!" He scooted over in the booth and nodded towards me. "Looks like I'm gonna have to teach my daughter here, too. Her mom done sissified her. Look at her, with her short hair and t-shirt." He shook his head in disgust.

"Detroit! You have a kid? You never talked about 'em." Sue smiled at me.

"Well, her momma took off when she got pregnant. Didn't even know she existed until Max here called me one day, wanting to come meet me." Detroit picked up his coffee cup with his bony, dirt-stained hands and slurped the last bit that hadn't spilled.

"Well, any kid of Detroit's is welcome here. What's your name?" Sue sat down next to me and put one hand on top of mine. Her hands, porcelain white, with long, red fingernails were a stark contrast to my stubby, tanned fingers with chewed fingernails.

"Maxine, I go by Max." I looked at her, suspicious of her motives.

"Well, Max, welcome to Wasco. Your breakfast is on the house. You got a beau? My oldest is about your age, may have to fix you up." Sue patted my hand.

"No mam, I don't. I don't date....." I stuttered.

"Never mind her, Sue, that's a damn good idea fixin' her up with that Jack of yours. Every girl in the county wants to go out with him. Captin' of the high school football team and all." Detroit slapped the table as if he'd just made everything perfect.

I just looked down at my lap, twisting my hands, wanting to run out of there and go home. I came on this trip to gain some self- reliance, to feel like an adult capable of making my own choices and accepting the consequences of those choices. I wanted the adventure of the unknown. I wasn't ready to settle down. There was a whole wide world beyond my sheltered life, and I wanted to experience it. If I had only known what was going to happen.

"Yeah, Max, you'll stay at my place tonight and we'll double date, me and my babe, Franny, and you and Jack, we'll have a great time!" Detroit took a big mouthful of his pancakes and shook his head with pride.

I was so excited that Dad wanted me to stay at his place, and more that he wanted to introduce me to his girlfriend and go out together. I thought he just needed to get to know me. I guess I lived a shielded life.

****

I'm still shaking two days after that night at Detroit's. I'd say calling him Dad is off the table. I may have some of his genes, like my curly hair, brown eyes and lanky frame, but I'd say nurture won out over nature. It's a bit sickening to think there are parts of him in me. Maybe we all have bad parts, we just choose whether to subject others to them.

I really don't want to write this down, but it feels important. I've come to realize that maybe seeking the past is the wrong direction, it won't help me to know myself. I've got to move forward, and experience what's ahead of me, to know what I'm made of. Nonetheless, this experience did help me to realize that I was mentally strong, and I could stand my ground. Otherwise, this could've gone a lot worse. Here's what happened on the 'date.'

Detroit didn't waste any time setting me up with Jack. He told me to go hang at his place while he worked, then we'd hang out that night.

Well, I found out pretty quickly why he never even bothered to lock his doors. His place looked like a frat house the morning after a big party. All that was missing was the Greek letters out front. I couldn't even sit inside. The smell of stale beer and cigarettes was just too much. Sure, I went to some frat parties at college, but not while I was sober. His couch was ripped up, I don't think he had ever changed his bedsheets-and the bathroom! Well, let's just say I relieved myself in his yard. Dug a little cat hole and everything, just like when I'm in the woods. I couldn't fathom touching anything in that house.

He got home about 7 pm. Those ranch hands put in long days in the summer, I guess. He looked like he'd been wrestling the cows instead of rounding them up. I know nothing about ranching and Detroit wasn't in the talking mood.

"Get some nice clothes on...." Detroit commanded me, "Franny and Jack be over any minute with some BBQ from Roadhouse. You ain't tasted BBQ until you've had their BBQ. They gets them pigs and cows fresh from our ranch and slaughters them right there in the yard." He mimicked cutting his throat. "Freshest BBQ you'll ever get. I got us some Jim Beam and PBR. Hope you don't drink that fancy stuff." Detroit raised up a fifth of Jim Beam and a twelve-pack of Pabst.

I shook my head. They both sounded awful, but I didn't plan to drink, anyway. I had never been much of a drinker.

I went out to my van and dug through my clothes. I wasn't sure what to wear that Detroit wouldn't make fun of. So, I just put on jeans and a cotton shirt. I wasn't packed for dressing up.

Detroit shrugged when I came back into the house. "Well, if that's the best you got. I doubt Jack cares much about what you wear. He doesn't seem to be too picky about his girls."

I wasn't sure what that meant but left it at that.

In the next second, the door opened, and in walked a woman who looked dressed to walk the streets of LA at night. At least from what I'd seen in the movies. Behind her trailed a young man with a crew cut, plaid shirt mostly open, and well-worn cowboy boots. He stood looking up and down my body like we were in a butcher shop. I wanted to run out then, but it was like there was something in me wanting to please my dad. I wanted him so much to say he was proud of me or something. I just kept telling myself it would help my relationship with Detroit. I thought if I just endured this 'date,' then he'd actually want to get to know me, not just my sexual preferences. I was out driving around to get to know myself better, and that I did.

Detroit's girl, Franny, had enough makeup on to cover several faces. She wore a red sequined dress that barely covered her butt-something Dad was pretty excited about.

Jack strutted right over to me, hugged me, and kissed me on the lips.

"Hi, I, I, I'm Max," I sputtered as I reached out my hand and tried to push him back.

Jack just laughed. "Detroit, your girl got some nice manners here." He turned his head back toward my dad.

"That's good. Maybe you can teach her some other things." Detroit winked at Jack like I wasn't standing right there. They all laughed. I wanted to vomit.

"Let's eat!" Detroit shouted as he patted Franny's behind.

I only needed a fork to eat the flavorful BBQ. It took me back to the cookouts we used to have with my mom and our friends from the Food Coop. I'd only been out on this soul-searching journey for a week, but I missed the comfort of the known, and people who accepted me. I closed my eyes remembering how much we laughed and sang. My favorite song to try to sing was John Denver's *The Eagle and Hawk*. Everyone would groan when I asked that we sing it, but everyone loved the challenge of trying to get to the high notes or sounding like the violins strumming. Memories like this made me question why I left my hometown. What was the urge that I felt to travel in my van for a few months instead of staying where I had family and friends? Franny's high pitch laugh roused me out of my brief reverie.

After we ate, Jack, Detroit and Franny started shooting shots of whiskey chased by beer. They kept teasing me, trying to get me to join in. Detroit grabbed my hand and forced some whiskey down my throat till Franny told him to leave me alone.

Another moment when I should've known to run.

And yet I stayed. *Why did I stay?*

They all started dancing around and Jack was rubbing all over me, sliding his tongue up and down my face and into my mouth.

"Jack, I'm gay." I said as I tried to put some distance between our bodies.

"Well, I'm feeling pretty good myself there, Max," he said with a lopsided grin.

He just kept movin' his body all around on me. Whenever I tried to sit down, he'd pull me back up. Not sure where Detroit and Franny went- they disappeared after the first song.

"No, Jack, I like girls. I date girls," I insisted. I kept pushing him away. He just laughed and grabbed me again.

"Well, just give me a few minutes and I'll change your mind about that."

Then he started unzipping my pants.

"No, Jack, really, please don't!" I tugged at my zipper and fought to keep my pants on.

"Oh, come on, Max, no one wants to come out and play?"

"Jack, please can we just talk? Tell me about your work."

He put his hand on my crotch and rubbed up and down and whispered, "Sure, talk about anything you want."

"Where do you work?" I sputtered out.

"Across town at the bar," he murmured.

He started putting his hand in my pants.

"Jack, please stop!" I yelled, grabbing his hand and throwing it back at him.

Was I being date raped?

He looked me in the face, full of surprise and anger. "What's wrong with you? There's a hundred girls out there that want me right now. I don't have to put up with this shit!" He picked up his beer and stomped toward the front door. "'Franny, I'm leaving, gonna go find me a real woman!" He slammed the door and was gone.

I just wrapped my arms around my legs, on the verge of tears. But it didn't feel safe, not there. I wanted a shower so badly. But I wanted out of that filth more.

Neither Detroit nor Franny said anything in response to Jack's words, so I tiptoed out to my van, locked the doors and crawled into my sleeping bag, trying to shake off the disgust and fear. I was so tired; I didn't feel like I should drive. He could've really hurt me, and my dad didn't care. I wrapped my sleeping bag around me tight, trying to hide from the pain. I don't know how long I'd been out, when the yelling started.

Detroit started pounding on my van window. "Girl, what the fuck is wrong with you? How could you scare off a boy like Jack? He'd fuck a rock if he could."

"Dad, I told you I like girls." I screamed from under my sleeping bag. Why did I call him that?

"You wait here, I'm gonna knock that shit right out of you."
Detroit pounded off toward the house.

I didn't wait to find out what that meant. I squirmed out of my sleeping bag and peered out my front van windows, looking for any sign of Detroit. When I didn't see him, I jumped in the driver's seat, turned the key, and sped off down the gravel driveway. I drove as fast as I could until I was well outside town. The adrenaline kept me going for most of the night. I'd been saving money for this trip for over a year, and I was already questioning my choices.

I can't believe that guy is my dad, biologically anyway. I sure hope I don't have any of his traits. I'm pretty rough and tumble compared to most girls my age, but that? How's it possible mom was ever with that guy? *I'm not sure I wanna' know.*

Made it up to Wichita Falls, Texas. All I could think of was, *Go north!* I really wanted to drive home. But I was being pulled back to New Mexico. I'd felt called to go on this journey, and I knew I hadn't gotten an answer yet.

One thing I learned from meeting Detroit, I was done longing for what could've been. Maybe things are the way they are for a reason. I was done trying to right a perceived wrong. I wanted to move forward and see where the road took me. I had no inkling of the new life it was leading me to.

I'll never regret that I listened to that inner tug.

Sara

"Where is she?" My brother Brian slammed open the screen door, shattering the peaceful afternoon.

"Sara! Where the hell are you?! I'm so tired of you embarrassing me!!" He was stomping all over the worn wood floors below my room. "You've done it again in the worst way." He seemed to just be shouting into the air. "I thought you'd normaled up, but nooooo! You gotta go around talking about trees speaking to you, and needing to protect the woods to a LOGGING company!!" He banged his fist against a wall.

"Brian, calm down." Mom had been reading on the porch swing. Brian hadn't even noticed her as he whizzed by. She was trying to talk calmly, but I knew she was as scared of Brian as I was.

It gave me chills to think of what he was capable of. Somewhere along the way Brian lost any compassion. Dad probably beat it out of him. I couldn't really blame Brian for how he was, but that was so long ago, Dad died and Mom had been loving towards him. Why wasn't that enough?

I couldn't begin to understand his pain, but it didn't make me any less frightened.

There was a time when he took care of me, protected me from the school bullies, but when the Dittons offered to pay for my college and then they had a job ready for me when I graduated, that was it. They'd never offered to pay for him to go to college.

Our relationship became cold and distant after that. It hurt. I tried so hard for him not to be jealous of me. I hid myself. I stayed distant and in the woods so that he could shine.

But he never really did. He focused on me with his jealous rage. "You get everything you want. People just hand you stuff. I hate you, you brat!"

It was a knife in my heart. I wasn't special. I didn't know why things came so easily to me, they just did.

"I'm sorry, Mom. I tried to keep him from coming here," said my younger brother, Joey, "If I didn't drive him here, he was going to drive himself, and that seemed even worse."

Joey always quivered behind Brian. Like he had an invisible umbilical cord attached to him, and Brian was what gave him life. After all the years I've known Joey, I know nothing about him. I only know what he mimicked in Brian. I felt sorry for him.

I yelled down from the top of the stairs, not knowing if it was safe to go down. "Brian, I've done nothing to you. I've told the truth, whether or not anyone believes it." I'd been writing an article hoping to explain things to the community. I wasn't sure that the local paper would publish it, but I had to at least try. Word had gotten around that I was trying to leave "perfectly good trees," when I worked for Ditton's, and I'd become the talk of the town.

I could smell Pabst Blue Ribbon Beer leaking out of Brian's tanned pores at the bottom of the stairs. PBR was his favorite beer, even though he could afford better. He'd been wearing his favorite trucker hat since he started hauling logs, 15 years ago. It was more dirt color than anything else now. I wasn't even sure I remembered what color his hair was. I never saw him without that thing.

"Sara!!" Brian raised his hand toward me, like he was mimicking what Dad used to do to him. "I'm so sick of your shit! Why can't you just be normal? Why do you have to go acting like you're all special and wanting attention?"

Funny-he thought I did this for attention. This kind of attention I didn't need or want. Ever since I'd been fired, you'd think I'd slept with everyone's husband or something. If I went into a store, people started whispering or shushing their voices. People I'd known all my life, and I considered family, now would barely talk to me.

"Brian, come over here and sit down. Let me get you some coffee." Mom patted the rocking chair in the corner of the screened in porch. The one that Mema used to rock us in and sing lullabies. I had to fight to hold back the tears. I wished Mema was here. She'd stand up for me, she'd make everyone shiver in their boots for ever thinking bad about me.

My mema was my hero. Nothing bothered her. She was completely confident in her ability to figure out anything. People and animals loved her equally and she loved them. Mema made all their clothes-and could smoke a deer with equal skill.

"Mom! You stay out of this!" Brian's voice was slurred. "This is between Sara and me! I'm so sick of you protecting her and giving her everything she wants." He continued to stare at me from the bottom of the worn oak stairs, daring me to come down. "She's gone too far with this! She's made me the laughingstock of the whole damn company! You should hear what they're saying...." His voice fell away and I almost felt sorry for him. There was barely enough light in the stairwell for me to make out his gristly brown beard that filled half his face. His plaid shirt was barely big enough to cover his belly.

Mom put out a hand. "Brian, I'm not protectin' anybody, I just don't see a need to fight, especially in your condition."

She lowered her voice, but not enough I couldn't hear. "Joey, would you go get him some coffee and water, please? And bring some of my pie and plates for everyone. There's nothing a fresh peach pie can't fix." The shaking in her voice betrayed her words. Mom and her cooking. She always believed it made everyone better.

I wished it was that simple.

When my grandpa built this house, he started with the screened in porch and added from there. There were big windows that looked out onto the porch from anyplace downstairs, this allowed Mema to see her beloved trees even from the top of the stairs. I couldn't have been more appreciative of this fact as I was right now. Seeing those trees gave me strength, when my knees were trying to melt.

"Mom, I'm not gonna sit and listen to Brian chew me out when I did nothing wrong, I'll be in my room." Clem, who'd been sitting next to me at the top of the stairs, voicing a low growl, almost ran me over getting back through my bedroom door.

Brian took two steps up the stairs and continued yelling. "Oh, no you don't, Miss. I don't give a shit about anybody else. You need to listen to me. You go back there and tell those people you're sorry and you made it all up." He pounded on the solid oak railing. "I will not have people laughing at me because of you!" I don't know what force kept him from coming all the way up, but I was grateful.

I shouted down, as Clem cowered to my room. "That's your problem, Brian. I will not apologize. I did nothing wrong." The more my brother yelled, the more confident I felt.

"Oh, come on, Sara." Mom was scooting around the kitchen getting plates and coffee. "What could it hurt to apologize, just so everyone gets along again?"

My mom, always the appeaser. She just wanted everyone to get along and play nice, no matter how much it meant burying who you were.

"No, Mom!!" I yelled. "I've been told to get along with everyone else my whole life! And I'm sick of it!" I started down the stairs to face my accusers head on. "I'm tired of being the way everyone else thinks I should. Nobody listens to me, no one gives a damn what I have to say, and I'm sick of it!" I ran down the stairs, right past Brian. As I passed my mom, I blurted, "I did nothing wrong!"

As I headed out the screened porch door, tears streamed down my face. I just wanted the pain to stop. I just wanted someone to care what I had to say. To hear and believe me for once. I ran through the tree shadows and out to the dock so the stars could blanket me with their knowing and under-standing.

I curled up with my knees to my chest. "Please help me. Please, why doesn't anyone care?" My body trembled on the hard surface of the dock.

It suddenly felt like someone was staring at me. I cocked my head up and found the piercing yellow eyes of a great gray owl staring into me from his perch in a spruce tree.

I covered my ears and lowered my head. "No! Don't talk to me! I pleaded. "Everyone thinks I'm nuts! Please go, please go talk to them, so they know, so they can hear you too!"

"They couldn't hear me even if I tried to talk with them, Sara." His voice was soft like a baby's coo.

"I don't care!" I shook my head. "Please go away! I can't take it anymore! I just can't take people making fun of me, calling me names! It hurts, it hurts too much. Please, please go away and stop talking to me." My stomach clenched as I sobbed the words.

He didn't leave. He stayed there, silent, as if to comfort and protect me should Brian come looking for me.

Sometime later the moon's rays woke me up, and the owl was still silently there. I didn't know what to do. I was scared to go back to the house, so I curled under the branches of a nearby pine tree and went back to sleep with the smell of sap and dirt filling my nostrils.

Maxine

I'm afraid to choose a direction. I thought going to see my dad was a good idea, but it was a nightmare. I don't trust myself anymore. I came out here to find myself and I feel like I've lost myself. I thought meeting my dad would help me know myself better, but that's a part of me I'd rather not know.

Everything I know is crumbling, even my steps feel like I'm walking on an earthquake.

After my mad rush to get away from Wasco, I find myself in this expanse of desert in southern New Mexico. The high desert of the Southwest is like nothing I've ever experienced. There's a hush, like no other. In Idaho, there's always a sound, even in the woods. The birds singing, the wind whispering in the tree leaves; the ground crunching. But in the desert, there's a hum, like the ground itself is singing. The quiet is so loud it's almost deafening.

The soil is so fragile. Every little plant struggles for life, making the most of the few spits of rain it gets. I hate walking on the earth, knowing it could be hundreds of years before the plants could come back. Even digging my morning cat hole feels like I was killing the ground. I'm gonna get a bucket. You can't leave toilet paper here. It'd never degrade in this dryness.

I'm glad Uncle Pete taught me about leaving no trace. It really disgusts me to see others toilet paper lying about.

I can see for miles in this place. I'm not sure where I am, just went down some dirt road on government protected land.

The STARS!! I had no idea there were so many stars!!

Last night I sat in my camp chair and asked the stars. "Which way do I go?" I didn't know why. It just felt like they knew everything. They'd been burning brightly for a lot longer than me.

I'd never experienced so much space and so many directions before. I never realized how comforting the known is. Having some limits on possibilities strangely feels more freeing than having infinite choices. When there are no limits, my brain seems to just go haywire.

It took three days in the quiet, humanless world, before I started feeling the invisible path and got an inkling it even existed. Before that, I'd felt empty and compassless.

My body slept and woke up with the sun's schedule. I was tired of the heat, so I looked for a way to keep cool in the desert oven. They said the monsoons would start in a couple of weeks and cool things off, but I wasn't seeing much but a few lingering clouds. At least it wasn't humid like at home.

My GPS showed some streams. For two days I chased those dotted blue lines on the map. I just kept going down dirt roads that took me toward the promised wet. Well, turns out that dotted blue lines must mean temporary places of water, not an actual stream. I saw very few solid blue lines on my map, the Rio Grande to the east being the main one. On and on I kept going, looking for the promised land until I was scorching hot. So I gave up and sat in my minivan. I'm embarrassed to admit it, but I just sat there in the middle of the desert with my air conditioner running, dunking my feet in a bucket of water. I'm the person who carries her bath water out to water the plants, but I didn't know how else to keep cool, and it just felt like it wasn't time for me to leave.

On the third morning, I felt compelled to look at my maps again. And that time I saw a little blue dot, with all these dotted lines converging toward it not too far away. I don't know how I missed it before. *Maybe it was a watering hole!*

I guess you're wondering why I didn't just get the hell out of there and drive someplace cooler, and I'll tell ya', I don't know. Something in me just said I needed to be there. I'd made a choice to come down this way, I felt like I needed to stop being the kid always seeking safety and comfort and start being an adult, who was responsible for my actions. I wasn't sure I liked this adult stuff so much.

That blue dot held great promise. I never imagined the secrets it was holding. Pearl's gas tank was full, and I had time, so I went to find out.

I zipped down this desert dirt road like I was headed to a restaurant after not eating for weeks. I just felt like this had to be it. There had to be some coolness there. If nothing else, at least some trees!

So I drove and drove. I felt like I was never gonna get there. You ever notice how long it seems to take when you're headed to someplace you wanna go, and how quickly you get back? What is that?

As I converged on the blue dotted lines, there it was, there was what I was looking for, only I didn't know it. Not trees, but an oasis sprouted up in the middle of the parched dirt. The moist smell lined my nostrils, and my cracked skin drank in the droplets of moisture that hung in the air. In an area about 100 feet in diameter was a vibrant green of small leafed bushes and inch high grasses. I wished I knew their names. I couldn't imagine what the animals would think when they came to this. If it hadn't been for that map, I would've thought I was still sleeping or the heat had scrambled my brain.

I'll forever be grateful to my college friend Aaron, who introduced me to spelunking, because there amid this desert, where flatness ruled the day, was some old igneous rock (think lava flow) that had gotten kicked out of the earth and exposed to the sun. As if to be able to breathe, a small hole, about three feet in diameter, opened above the ground and provided an oasis for some persistent plants to thrive. The little blue dots of water the satellites were picking up were underground!

I was concerned about who else, or what else might live in the cave, so with my walking stick I went to within a foot of the whale mouth entrance and yelled, "Anybody home! Anybody home?!" Then hurried back to my car. I hoped that was enough to pry any homesteaders loose.

Nothing, not so much as a lizard came out.

I felt trepidation about heading into a cave by myself, but my curiosity won out. So, I grabbed my headlamp, and laced up my hiking shoes. I felt pulled into that cave. My feet were going whether or not I followed. When I got to within a foot of the opening nirvana came rushing out, like a fire hydrant on a city's summer street. My whole body tingled and shook out the heat.

The light from my headlamp lit up the shimmering crystal-like walls. My shoulders dropped and my lungs took in a deep gulp of the damp air. A part of me wanted to lick the moist walls and plaster my body against the cool rock. But the invisible rope that was pulling me in, tugged at my heart. For the first time in my life, I was glad I was short. I took a deep breath, ducked my head, and crawled on the earth-covered hard, cold, surface into the dark.

If you've never crawled through a hole in the earth, imagine you're a baby trying to get back to where you were before you were born. You have to contort yourself, and slink along the damp surfaces. It felt natural to go into the earth's womb. Luckily, I'm not claustrophobic.

I inched along on the rocky, slick surface, peering at every inch my headlamp lit up, and looking for critters who called this home. My climbing rope, hanging across my shoulder, hampered my movements. I wasn't planning on doing any rappelling, but Aaron had taught me that it's good to have a rope in case you fall into an abyss.

The cave slowly sloped into the earth. The dirt became grainy mud, and water dripped from the sculpted walls. I heard a familiar faint bubbling in the distance. Just what I wanted, someplace to get wet! So, I continued on my hands and knees, inching my way along the rock and mud floor. I was grateful for the strong arms, years of swimming had given me. Going slowly in an unknown space like this is important. You never know when you may stumble upon something a light doesn't expose.

I inched my right hand, then left knee, my left hand, then my right knee. Letting the invisible rope take me further into the earth's depths. I just kept reminding myself to breathe, as my heart raced. *What if something blocks the entrance? What if I get lost?* I tried to control the panicky thoughts. But they were valid questions.

All along the shimmering brown walls and ceiling were little nooks and crannies, great places for a kid to hide his treasures from his little brother. I'd always wished I had a brother or sister to play games with. I didn't dare put my hands on any of them as I feared the only treasure I'd find was a snake, or worse, a scorpion!

In the dark, going 20 feet, seems to take an hour. Even with a light, every movement is measured and assured. The sound of the gurgling water got closer and closer. In mid stride, my headlamp lit up another dark cavern about 3 feet in diameter that worm-holed into the earth. It was symmetrical and smooth from centuries of flowing water. Going around it would have taken more finesse than I had. After shining the light all along its edges and the ground beneath me, I slowly lowered onto my belly. I gently pulled my upper body to the edge of the hole and let my headlamp light up the source of the gurgling. About 10 feet down in the dark, waters flowed along a mysterious underground path. The earth was filled with these hidden rivers, and every now and again, they showed themselves in little caves.

Wow! I wonder if the people and animals know about this! I draped over the ledge hoping for a way to crawl down to the soothing water. But I found something so much better.

My headlamp hit upon an unnatural shininess. It was so alien in this environment that I couldn't tell what it was at first. I tentatively lowered the top of my body over the edge of the vertical shaft to get a closer look.

But once I saw what it was, my body deflated. *Great, trash! Some moron left his trash in this pristine cave!*

I reached in the back pocket of my jeans and pulled out my leather gloves. I took a deep breath, hung back over the edge and gently tugged at one corner of the plastic bag. Millimeter by millimeter, my outstretched arm reeled in the bag. I prayed with all my heart that nothing would come spilling out.

Was there more?

Once the plastic blob was safely at my feet, I lowered my upper body back over the ledge and looked for more trash or a way to get down to the stirring waters. I didn't see either. I just stared into the translucent black waters, watching streaks of tiny fish dart about. We'd seen them before in caves. Aaron said they were blind, for obvious reasons. It always bewildered me. *How did they get there? What did they eat?* The glistening walls of the vertical tunnel were mesmerizing. I so wanted to go in, but thought I'd wait for Aaron to come along with me one day.

It was only when I went to tuck the plastic bag in my back pocket that I noticed it had a rectangular thing inside. It made carrying it out a little more challenging, but there was no way I was gonna leave trash behind. I crawled back towards the light, from the day's scorching sun, pouring into the entry and sat at the cave's mouth. My body shivered and my mouth smiled. My cells woke up from the cold caffeine. I didn't get the hoped for bath, but I was cool.

Maxine

I didn't have any better ideas, and at least I knew I had a cave I could crawl into during the heat of the day, so I stayed about ¼ mile from the cave that night. I wanted to give room for any critters that may go there to lap the water from the seeping walls.

In the still cool morning, I put out my camp chair with its back to the sun and clipped my umbrella to the chair. This would give me a little extra cool and keep the sun from giving me any more freckles. I carefully lifted the plastic bag off the passenger seat and sat down in my chair. I peered at the object inside the bag. It looked like a book. I was a bit concerned I'd found someone's secret diary and I was about to pry.

I carefully undid each layer of plastic and put the twist tie inside each bag. I felt like I was unwrapping a sacred object. Who knows? It might be just a bunch of random scribbles, but I was feeling all bubbly inside, like I was opening a whole new world.

After all the bags were off, a notebook lay in my lap. Working diligently to keep it in the shade, I opened the thin cardboard cover and read the first words:

"Hi! If you find this, please take good care of it. If you can't do that, I hope you'll put it back. I don't know what I expect you to do with the information in these pages, but I just felt someone else had to know. I'm hoping the person who finds this is the exact right person to do something with what I learned and that they will have more courage than I had to share it with others."

It was a small, artistic looking handwriting. Definitely a woman's.

I sat down to read about 8 am, and next thing I knew, the sun was staring me in the face burning my skin. It was noon. I finished the notebook all at once.

The pathways in my brain were acting like a summer thunderstorm. *What did I do with all this information?*

I carefully put the frail notebook back in the plastic bags that had guarded it all these years and placed it under the passenger seat of my van to protect it from the scorching sun.

I grabbed my head lamp and headed to the cave.

This time, I just sat within 10 feet of the entrance. It was cool there, and I wanted to mull over what I had read and think about my next steps. I hadn't done much contemplating before my thoughts were disrupted by a coarse voice.

"Hello! Hello! Anybody in there?"

My heart jumped.

"Of course someone's in there, Frank. Where else would they be?" said a slightly smoother woman's voice. Both voices sounded scratchy, like they had a lot of years on those vocal chords.

What if I wasn't supposed to be here? I thought to myself.

I called out, "Um, yes, yes sir, I'm in here. Max is my name. I'll come right out." Shaking, not knowing what I was getting myself into, I crawled out through the earth's mouth. The sun shocked my eyes. I covered my face and stood up, trying to look at the people through my fingers.

"Well, high ya,'" the gruff voice said. "Max, sure a strange name for a girl. Found our cooling spot, did ya?" The white-haired man in worn jeans and a long- sleeve shirt leaned toward me.

"I'm sorry if I'm trespassing, sir." My trembling hands continued to haphazardly cover my eyes.

"Oh no, this is public land, just hadn't seen anyone else here since Sara left. Always happy to have company." He reached out a hand and showed his crooked brown teeth.

My hands fell to my sides, and my eyes widened despite the glare."You talkin' about Sara that wrote the notebook?"

"Did Sara write a notebook, honey?" The man looked at the gray-haired woman smiling beside him.

"I think so, Frank. She was always scribbling in that thing under the elm tree by the barn." The woman's eyes looked into the past. "Didn't know she'd left it here, though." She peered at me. "Where'd you find it?"

"In the cave." I nodded toward the cave entrance. "I was trying to get to the water, and I found it on a ledge of the tunnel that goes down to that creek in there." I pointed to the invisible ledge.

"Wow! All the years we've been comin' here and never saw that thing!" The woman elbowed the man.

"Well, I saw somethin' on that ledge, but I just left it alone," Frank offered. "No one else ever out here but Alice and me. Sure hope you don't put the cave on that internet or something. Then there'll be swarms of people. Don't need that." Frank creased his brows at me.

"No sir, I won't do that." I shook my head and tried to look trustworthy.

"Good. Well, did you read it?" The old man continued to squint at me.

"I did." I wasn't sure whether that was the right answer. "Her words and story touched me. Made me think about things a little differently. It felt like she was talking to me."

The woman's face became soft, and her eyelids lowered like she was reliving a fond memory. "Yes it is, isn't it? Sara's a special girl."

"So you know?" My ears perked up. "When was she here? Why was she here?" I had to stop myself from firing too many questions at them.

Alice slowly nodded. "Oh yeah, she came and stayed at our place. She was haven' a heck of a time with her brother. She just needed to get away and ended up at our place one day."

Frank looked at his wife and chuckled. "I'll never forget that morning she showed up at the house. She was looking at you like you were crazy. You were talking to her like you'd been best friends all your lives."

The woman returned her husband's smile. "Well, felt like we had."

"When was that?" I repeated.

Alice gazed up at the sky. "Well, what'd ya think, Frank? Twenty, thirty years ago?" Alice nodded to herself. "Yeah, that sounds about right, about 30 years ago. It was after she'd helped with a couple big fires. They had a big one near Rico, just north of here, so she came down this way. She spent a lot of time writing and talking about what she was gonna do."

Frank nodded his head.

I asked what I really wanted to know. "Where is Sara now?"

The man looked sullen. "Sorry, Max, we haven't heard from her in some time. We always figured she'd end up back here one day, but nothin' yet."

"I really need to find her and talk to her about her story. It's really got my brain thinking differently about things."

"Well then, sounds like the right person found that notebook." Alice reached out her hand to me with a smile usually reserved for babies. "Mind if I look?"

"No, no! Please do!" I ran to the front seat of Pearl and gently lifted the plastic package.

Alice called after me. "I don't need to read it. I heard the story straight from the horse's mouth, ya' know, just haven't seen her handwriting in awhile."

I carefully unwrapped the diary and carried it to the woman's hands.

She just held it there as it rested on her palms, like she was praying to it. Then she placed her right hand on top of the notebook with her left hand still supporting it underneath. Her eyes remained closed the entire time, and her breath was light and easy.

After a few minutes, she opened her eyes and gently lifted the front cover. She smiled when she saw the first words. I don't think she read them, but she had seen the handwriting of a long-lost child, someone she had taken under her wing and let fly away when it was time.

She gingerly flipped a few more pages, glanced at the writing, brought the notebook to her chest, closed her eyes, and smiled. She wore a look of pride and exaltation. After a few stirring moments she removed the notebook from her chest and offered it back to me.

"Take good care of Sara's story," She whispered to me.

"I will." I murmured back as I cradled the notebook.

"Well, ladies," the man's voice broke the spell. "It's getting pretty hot out here. Why don't we continue this conversation in the cool cave?" He nodded toward the oasis.

The woman smiled, and headed to the rock opening. Frank and I followed behind.

I felt like the couple had broken the champagne bottle across my bow and I could head off into uncharted waters. I was giddy with excitement.

As we sat in the dark, soothing cave, with the sun's rays piercing the opening, I asked, "Do you have any idea how I find her?"

The woman placed one weathered hand over my heart and one hand below my sternum. "Listen here, just listen here.

They will lead you to where you want to go." She gazed deeply into my eyes.

I took a deep breath, laid my head back on the moist rock wall, and smiled.

I was on my way.

Sara

A few days had passed since I was fired.

I spent my time wandering around our 12,000 acre tree haven, lost in a conundrum. My Grandparents had settled this land a century ago. They'd never let it be logged. They figured nature knew how to take care of itself a lot better than people did. To them that would be like a monkey thinking it knew what a human needed. And the trees had been around longer than any people and would be here when the humans were long gone. They did let the occasional lightning-caused fire do its thing. Fire was nature's logging, the plants needed it. The property was filled with everything from big leafed thimbleberries to velvet-barked douglas fir. Having such a variety of species allowed me to choose from the comforting, shadeless trunks of the fir trees or the sun umbrellas of the red cedars.

I missed my mema. Her presence filled me with confidence, a light in the stormy childhood seas. I especially missed the stories she told me about floating people and talking trees. I thought she was making it up.

She found this property. Her intuition led her here, she said. She always said it was a special place filled with fairies and wood nymphs. I'm sure I saw them when I was a child.

The stream that ran through the acreage was like an umbilical cord to my beloved woods. It pooled into a large pond Grandad had made. The waters reminded me of what's real and important. It was liquid love. A love I'd never felt from another human, one I didn't think was possible.

I'd wandered every inch of that property. It was my skin. I felt what she felt, I heard what she heard. I knew when mama bear would show up with her cubs and where; I knew where the fawns would be hiding. I stayed clear of these areas during the times I knew they'd be there. Like me, they just wanted to be left alone by human beings. People were unpredictable, hurt others when they hurt, killed for no reason. At least that's all I knew then.

Since all her children worked for the logging company, Mom had a hard time explaining why they couldn't harvest her trees. They gave her all the reasons they believed it would be better to let them come in and 'clean up the place,' but Mom just smiled, shook her head and said, "you just don't get it."

At that point, she would scoot back her chair, pick up the cake and coffee she'd offered, and say, "Have a good day, gentlemen." And off she would go.

As a child, I loved watching this play unfold. Every year they'd come knocking, and every year they'd leave in disgust. They didn't get it. And it turns out I didn't get it either.

I thought she was protecting the trees. I didn't know then that I was about to discover what she was really protecting.

I leaned against Mother Tree, a 40-foot diameter Cedar tree. Her soft, red bark had comforted me since I was 5. She was the life of the party, the mom every kid wished was theirs. She invited everyone in and cared for them with her loving arms. Today she was a grounding rod as I followed the thread of what had gotten me here.

It was over two months ago. I was on a 3-week assignment when I first heard the voices in the forest. I thought it was Brian and Joey pulling a brotherly prank on me.

But then I heard them again, that night, dreaming under a blanket of stars. The forest was sleeping, the breeze was resting, no animals were scurrying around. It was the type of quiet that gave me chills as I felt the perfection of everything. I felt like one of the trees-that I could just melt into the earth. I felt connected to who I truly was, like I was the dirt itself.

I was reveling in the feeling of being wrapped in love by the stars when out sprung from my lips a whispered, "thank you."

"Thank you for noticing," a voice responded. It was a little different tone than before. It was more like a smiling child proud of her drawing.

This time, I didn't look around. I knew there wasn't anyone there or Clem would bark. He didn't say much, but he did bark at night if we had visitors. Instead, he stayed curled up next to me with his head on my stomach, breathing gently. In the quiet, I could feel there was nothing to fear. The sound was so natural.

It did worry me a bit. *Was I losing it? Did anyone else hear the voices?* But they were the softest voices I'd ever heard. Like someone singing a lullaby. They just said how much they loved me. There was no judgment about what I was doing. Even when I'd mark the tree trunks for cutting, they were a lover whispering honeyed words into my ear. I just didn't get it. *Why me?*

The voices were always there but not like the obtrusive sound of people talking in the woods. *Was this what drew people to the woods? Did it remind us of being in a womb and hearing our mother's crooning voice and not knowing what it was? The melody, comforting and significant. Do we know in our bones the voice gives us life even when we don't know how?*

After a while, I figured out that it was mostly the trees talking to me. Though sometimes the animals or other plants did too. Sometimes it was individual trees, sometimes a chorus. They made suggestions on what trees to not mark, and why it was important to leave the older trees. They told me about how interconnected all the plants were. I saw in my mind's eyes a network running below the surface of the earth. It reminded me of what I imagined the neural pathways in our brain looked like. Only these pathways connected all the plant life. They all shared information and water no matter if it was the biggest spruce or the smallest meadow rue.

I came to really love hearing them at night. I could ask about something in my mind, and they would answer. They were the antennae to universal knowledge, bringing God's knowledge to earth so we humans could pick it up in the foods we eat and the waters we drink. It was like having a wise mentor always listening. I would often lie awake at night just to look at the stars and ask the trees questions.

Now, I was once again turning to Mother Tree for answers, as I had before I heard her talk.

I'd reached the edges of sorrow and frustration. "I've let everyone down, and now I'm letting you down," I whispered to the trees. I wondered how I couldn't have heard them all these years until now. Now they were loud in a calming way, soothing like a heartbeat and rain on the roof after months of drought.

"My dear love." The sound was like a wispy cloud. "You haven't let us down. You're doing the best you can."

"I don't think I am. I feel like an idiot." I shook my head and yelled. "I'm scared, so scared of leaving the box they've put me in. The box that I've stayed in. Even though it feels like a fiery hell."

"What would happen if you tore down the box?"

When I heard them, it was like the moon singing soft, sweet words. I could only hear them when it was quiet. I could be walking or sitting under a tree. But I had to give them space or the chatter of my mind would drown their whispering out.

"I'd be all alone. Lost in an abyss of starless black."

"We'd be here."

"Yes, but you can't hug me when I'm sick. You can't care for Clem when I'm gone. Those people are my friends, my family, the only way of life I've ever known, and they don't like me any way than the way they've known me." Tears streamed down my cheeks.

I needed someone to thrash this out with and I could count on them to hear me without judgment. Clem caught a whiff of something and wandered off to investigate.

"My dear Sara, there's nothing you can do about that." Their voices seemed so focused, so full of love and safety, and yet in stereo, surrounding me.

She was right, this airy voice. I'm certain it was Mother Tree, but it could've been the squirrel across the creek. The thing about these voices is that everything they said felt so sure, so real, like they were speaking to my soul, the place in me that knows everything.

Wetness blurred my vision. I pulled my knees to my chin and held tight around my calves. It had been a dry June. The ground was crusty, and the plants were struggling to poke through. The moisture smell had been rung out of the air by the bright sun, leaving dust to fill my nostrils. It was the driest I'd ever seen it.

I choked out, "you make it sound so easy, but it's not fair! Why do I have to choose between them and being who I am?"

"My love, it's human nature for people to want you to believe like they do." The voices were always confident and kind. It was like a steady stream of water that melted my nervousness.

"When you say it, it makes so much sense, it's so normal. But I don't know how to change after all these years. What should I do? Where do I go? How do I get them to be okay with who I really am?"

Right then, a mature bald eagle landed in a bare branch far above my head with a crackling grace. It was as if someone had just put an angel atop my Christmas tree.

'You don't,' said her voice with a quiet shrillness. "It's not their responsibility to be okay with you. You're not even okay with you. You're still ashamed of being able to hear us, what you know in your bones, and what you see."

A crack in my facade crevassed. "You make it all seem so easy! Why doesn't anybody ever listen to me!" I stood up, yelling at the top of my lungs. "There's no way you can understand how I feel. You're a bird! No one expects anything from you!" Years of caged words spewed out as my arm flung rocks onto the defenseless soil.

One particular rock suffered the brunt of my anger, as I hurled it over and over to the ground beneath me. The air was my punching bag, and it felt so unsatisfying.

The energy unfurled from deep within me, so erratic and scary. I'd never let myself feel all this. It never felt safe.

"ARRRRRRRR!!!" I was yelling and feeling shame at the same time. "I hope no one can hear me." That was my life in a sentence. Fearing my words, fearing my feelings, because repeatedly, others sideswiped them. I was told to move on, told to rein them in.

I screamed as loud as my throat would allow. "What is wrong with people? Especially my family? Telling me not to feel the way I feel! I'm so sick of it!"

Time stood still around me, not another sound, not another breath. I wondered if the eagle was still there, witnessing my tantrum. I was embarrassed by my unruly behavior in front of such a stoic bird, so I didn't look.

I found more rocks to hurl, trying not to hit any plants. I felt empty, hollow to the core. The people who were to help guide me to myself, tried instead to put me in their mold. It's what they thought would keep me safe. Free from the ache of failure. Instead, it brought me loneliness because I didn't have my own guiding light. I only had theirs. It was like trying to fit a cat in a box. At some point I had given up fighting. Until now.

"I'm so stupid! How could I let so many people control my life, tell me what to do and not do? God, I really hate myself sometimes." I started punching out with my arms. I wanted to control my thoughts, I wanted to control my actions, but I had let my mind see the light and it had taken control.

For long minutes my two-year-old took the wheel and had her way. Screaming in baby wails, hitting the air and throwing rocks, until my 30-year-old body had nothing left to give. She became a gelatin mass and collapsed in a weeping heap on the dry grass.

I peered up from my horizontal plane and the eagle was still there. She'd stayed, she'd witnessed my terror, my rage, my years of pent-up holding, and she didn't say a thing. She didn't tell me I was wrong, or that there was something wrong with me for feeling that way. She just sat on her perch and looked out towards the pond. My eyes watered the soil, and the ground held me like a mother should. For the first time in my life, I felt like it was okay; I was okay, whatever I felt, whatever I said, no one was there to tell me it was wrong. My body shook out the last of the pain and despair, and I fell asleep.

I awoke as the sun was getting shaded by the lower trees, and she was still there. The eagle had stayed.

Where once was rage, was vast space. My body had no edges and I felt like the sun.

"Thank you," I whispered to my majestic friend.

She looked into my face, spread out her wings and her clawed feet released the branch as one big swoosh hurled her out of sight. The fogginess of sleep stayed draped over me, and I enjoyed the quiet within, the cooling ground, and the singing birds. For the first time since I'd started hearing the sounds, I started feeling supported and a flicker of hope lit up my heart.

And as if to seal the deal, a splash of water leapt up from the creek and kissed me on the cheek, leaving my arms and legs dampened.

Maxine

I awoke to another sun-filled morning. The older couple I'd met, Alice and Frank, invited me to stay at their farm near the cave. They hadn't planted anything in decades. Once the water stopped flowing in the fields, the cacti, creosote and brittlebush took over. The little irrigation ditch near the house kept the orchard producing and the grasses green there.

In the last few weeks, I'd gotten to where I woke up at 5 am just as the stars were going into hiding. I'd get out and do whatever chores I didn't finish the previous day, before the sun melted the cool. Frank joined me when he could. His shriveling muscles still popped up under his crinkly skin. He's 90 now, but not mentally ready to slow down. His body often has other ideas. But once he gets going, his momentum is like a rock sliding downhill. There's nothing to stop him. Except Alice. She comes out at noon each day, and hands out freshly baked chocolate chip cookies and squeezed lemonade. We always felt obliged to stop. It's then we'd notice how hot we were.

The monsoons are doing well this year, they say, best they've had in years. In the mornings the liquid cotton clouds meander and morph across the dense blue sky. They bloom into a billowing mass with dark underbellies and glowing sides. As the day heats up the clouds drop silk ribbons of water that sweep across the horizon. Makes for more work, but more green. They've been using buckets to gather the water from the leaky roof, but this year it required more buckets than they had. So I fixed the roof. I didn't know I could. Frank guided me from the ground. Frank and Alice look at me as if I can do anything. They make me feel I can do anything. They give me space to make mistakes and figure things out, always near to lend an encouraging hand.

Alice and Frank are like the grandparents I never had. I never even asked Mom why I'd never met my grandparents-or at least heard of them. At the co-op, I felt like I had a whole family of people. There was Uncle Ronny and Aunt Sue, and all the other employees we spent the holidays with, but I had no grandparent figures, until now.

Alice and Frank have lived out here for nearly 50 years. The house was filled with tarnished antiques and threadbare Persian rugs. When I asked where they got the rugs, Alice smiled. "Well, Persia, of course." Then they'd go back to doing whatever, like getting your rugs in Persia was what everyone did.

The antique furniture were things Alice had inherited, but there weren't any photos of the family around. I asked about a few sketches of various people Alice had done. "Oh, those are just scribbles," she told me. I loved my time with them. I felt useful and appreciated. It's one thing to feel that from your mom, but another to have complete strangers take you in.

***

"Max, we'd like to have a chat with you," Frank said. It was our daily lunch hour under a big cottonwood tree outside their back door. They seemed to have the only trees for miles. They said these trees were here when they bought the 400-acre parcel, and they just tucked the house in between them, careful not to disturb the roots or their water source. Their house definitely looked like they had made it to fit its exact spot with the kitchen facing east, to catch the morning sun filtering through the massive cottonwood branches.

Alice folded my hand in between hers and looked me in the eye. Her indigo eyes were always filled with warmth and gentleness. It was as if a stream of love and compassion always flowed out of them. I wondered how she did it.

"Max, it's time for you to move on, follow your intuition, and take the next steps."

I took a deep breath and let the air out slowly, carefully, as if when all the air was out, I was going to have to make a choice I didn't want to make.

Except I hadn't been given a choice, and I didn't want to feel what was behind that deep breath.

"You've been here for three weeks," she continued. "You were really excited to move on and find Sara, and we've held you back. You've been such a great help, like having a grandchild around. But the work around here will never stop, and it can't stop your journey." She smiled at me and continued to envelop my hands with hers.

Inside I screamed, "I don't wanna leave!! I LOVE it here! I'm not ready to go!" But I also knew she was right. My breath stuttered while I tried to find the words, words that wouldn't betray my confidence.

During my weeks with Frank and Alice, I began to feel like an adult. They showed me I could do anything I set my mind to. It was like I needed strangers to help me see who I really was, to point me in the direction and reflect it back to me. I was never their little girl who peed in her pants. I was an intelligent adult who they admired for shoving off from the dock and seeing where the tide took me.

Frank saved me.

"You can enjoy the rest of the day, and we'll get you fixed up with some sandwiches for the road. Then you leave at first light, while the cool is still your friend." I'd never heard his voice so low and fatherly.

I smiled, put down my ham sandwich and looked at the ants who joined our picnic. If I looked at the kindly couple, my fear would gush out. Alice gave a squeeze and let my hand join the other one. We ate the rest of our lunch quietly.

Later that afternoon, I went to the cave to cool off like I did every day. As my head leaned back on the slippery walls, I wondered, *what is wrong with me? The whole reason I came on this adventure was to get to know myself. Now I'm scared to leave, scared to embark on the unknown, and follow the stranger path.*

In her notebook, Sara talked about realizing that road-blocks often turned her down a better path. Maybe that's what is happening now. Frank and Alice kicking me out is the Universe's way of telling me it's time to leave, that the timing was perfect.

A little later, Frank joined me. "I know how you're feeling." he said, leaning against the opposite wall with our legs parallel.

I hadn't said a word.

"It's hard to leave the comfort and the known." He continued as if I had asked for more. "Most people never do. They grow up and live the life their parents had. Maybe a different address, different jobs and hobbies, but still the same. It's human nature to stay safe. It's how our ancestors survived all these years. But you can't make safety your goal- you'll lose that sense of aliveness. When I was about your age, I dreamed of leaving the family farm and starting an almond orchard in California. My Dad and I never saw eye to eye on how to grow things, and I wanted to go try things out. But I was scared of failing and not knowing anyone, so I stayed. I kept saying 'next year.' Then 1929 and the great depression hit. I couldn't leave my family then. I had to help us all survive. Frank got a dreamy look in his eye as he looked through the cave entrance. I don't know what would've happened had I left when I first had the idea. And that's the thing, I don't know. I'd rather have tried and failed than not know. I regret that I let fear and comfort guide me and not my dreams. I'm not talking bungee jumping or skydiving, I'm talking about leaving the security behind, being quiet in your own skin, not knowing a soul around you, getting challenged to your core and coming out the other side. That's what life really is. It took me a lot of years to realize this.

As soon as I could, I went to California. I couldn't get a job at an almond ranch. So I just took what jobs I could get until I found a job I loved. Which turned out to be flying. I had to try a lot of things before I found something that fit. But I learned a lot about myself in the process.

Now we make laws and rules to stay safe, and when you walk down the street or go to the grocery store, you see a bunch of zombies, people who are just walking in the muck, half dead inside even when their bodies are nowhere near a grave. Don't let that be you. Don't just read about adventures in books-create your own." He looked deeply into my eyes. "Yes, it's scary, but you'll never know what you're capable of until you try."

I wrapped my arms around my bent knees. I could feel my chest clinging to the edge of open and closed. I wanted so much to jump up and fly and yet my mind kept saying 'no! stay on the ground, it's nice and safe here. You won't get hurt.' I pondered as Frank sat with closed eyes across from me. *Is that what we're here to do? Just stay safe? We all love to watch the astronauts fly off, and the stunt pilots move in impossible ways. Is that our spirit telling us there's so much more?*

I watched my coworkers look at the astronauts and olympians with awe. They'd be glued to the TV when they were on. But watching people achieve their dreams left me feeling cold. I just couldn't stay and watch. It's easy to create excuses for not being a pilot or astronaut or Olympic-level athlete, right? That requires a lot of skills you need to be born with. But does that mean we don't pull off the comforter, unplug the TV, disconnect the cable and go somewhere where we aren't known?

I'd go hiking in the woods around Moscow and see people camped in their big motorhomes, satellite dishes pointed to the sky. It made me start wondering what camping meant to me. How did I want to live my life? I heard my backpacking friends talk about how much they loved the simplicity of carrying everything on their back. It made them realize how little they needed.

As I prepared for my trip, I contemplated what to bring and not to bring. To leave the familiar behind. To have a real adventure not just a semblance of one. There was so much I was certain I'd need. Yet, I'd found the less I had, the happier and freer I felt.

I didn't know the answers. And I certainly couldn't answer for everyone. But I knew I wanted more than a safe shell.

And here I was again, leaping into the great abyss. The memory of my last night in Moscow, Idaho, where I'd grown up, came streaming in.

A man I called Uncle Pete, sat me down the night before I left. I think he tried to be a father figure in my fatherless world.

He said, "Max, go with the flow out there. Don't be in a rush. Feel for the invisible brick road. It will lead you to where you want to go."

I didn't understand. I wasn't really going anywhere. But now I see how right he was. I'd just happened to meet these people, and I was a different person than I was when I met them. I could fix a screen window, and barn doors. Alice even taught me how to draw the things I see. They both gave me the space to figure things out on my own. They didn't question my judgment. Now I knew I could do anything I set my mind to. It may not be pretty, but at least I tried.

When I started this trip, I needed to figure out who I was when I wasn't around people I'd known all my life. Many find this in college, but I went to school in town. I got a degree in what others thought I was good at. My mom had worked hard to make sure I could go to college. She worked two jobs most of my life, one at the university, so I'd get free tuition. So she expected I'd go straight to college after high school, but I tell ya', I don't think I was ready.

So now, with the freedom of having graduated, I was taking some time off from the co-op where I'd worked since I was 12. I wanted to see what I was made of. I probably wasn't ready for the adventure I ended up on. Are we ever? As Uncle Pete said, "You can't wait for all the lights to turn green before you start across town." I was ten and trying to decide whether to join the swim team. I'd always loved swimming, but I didn't like competition. Well, that's what I thought. Turned out I loved competing against others, it made me push myself.

Frank's cough brought me back to the cave. I smiled at him. *I knew he was right. I'd forgotten.* It was time to be truly on my own, not just do what was in front of me, but to follow the quiet, my inner voice, and find more of myself.

The notebook was sitting under the front seat of Pearl. Waiting. One thing I knew for sure- I wanted to find out more about its writer.

Sara

I awoke the next morning at the base of a pine tree at the edge of the pond. The sun grazed the edges of the ridge, and its rays splashed into my eyes.

The owl that had visited me a couple days earlier sat grasping the branches above me, with his eyes closed. The shade darkened his mottled-gray feathers. The sun hadn't gotten over the hill yet, but its light shone through the dense forest. The black-capped chickadees and American Robin were praising the new day. Quiet enveloped the bird songs. I was on the verge of shivering, but it was soothing to my anger filled body.

"It's not your fault, Sara," he murmured as I stared up at him.

He startled me. I'd assumed he was asleep.

"What's that?" My voice was weak, and my eyes were puffy. I pulled my knees up to my chest. As much as I didn't want to hear the owl talk, he felt like one of my few friends now. Only the trees and animals truly saw and heard me. I guess I'm lucky. Many people don't have anyone who they feel really knows them.

"How Brian or anyone else behaves or feels. You've done nothing wrong," said the soft voice. It's hard to explain how the owl's speech is different from the tree's voice. They're all so quiet and matter-of-fact. The difference is only in degrees. They're similar, but with a slightly different tone. Also, there's directionality to the voice. I could tell it was the owl because it came from his direction.

"I know that at one level," I replied, grateful I had someone to talk to. "But my whole life, my parents, teachers, and brothers have said, "Sara, you're giving me a headache, Sara you're making me angry. Sara, why don't you just act like everyone else?" And it sucks. I know it's not my fault, but they don't seem to own their own feelings. And it hurts, it really hurts. Being in the woods is so much easier. When I'm around people I feel like I'm in a constant game of Russian Roulette. I just want it to stop!"

"I know. I'm sorry it hurts so much," the owl continued like the best therapist. "You feel everything so deeply. I know it's hard not to want to control how others feel too." He opened his eyes and quietly flew down to a lower branch. It was eerie how a bird the size of a cat could fly so quietly. Their feathers are specially designed for this so as not to scare their nighttime prey.

I put my hand on my forehead. "But it's not about wanting to control how others feel. I just want them to stop blaming me!" I took a deep breath of the tingly air and looked out to the glassy waters reflecting the surrounding trees. I knew he was trying to help.

"But that's what I mean," the owl continued from only a couple of branches above my head. "You can't stop people from blaming you for how they feel. It's just easier, it's human nature." His eyelids gently fluttered. "You get to stop trying to control what others feel. If those people want to blame others, they get to do that. You can't stop them."

I shook my head and wrapped my arms across my chest. "I just don't think I can take it anymore. I just feel empty rage inside, and I hate it. I really hate it." I looked back up at him, hoping my incensed words didn't scare him.

"I know, Sara. I'm sorry, so sorry." He continued to peer down into my eyes.

I got up, walked to the edge of the dock and sat with my legs dangling over the edge, toes strumming the water's surface. I just wanted to go back to the woods. It was so much easier when I could just stay out there and didn't have to deal with people. Everything was simpler. I was happier. Maybe I should've just kept my mouth shut instead of telling people about the trees. A part of me wanted things to go back to the way they were. But that wouldn't happen. No logging company would hire me now, and I didn't know what else I could do. Those are often the best moments. The moments when you let go. Then a power greater than us can take over and lead us to places we didn't even know existed.

I glimpsed a shiny rock on the far side of the pond. I'd swum in these waters since I was two weeks old, and I'd never seen the rock down there. I took off my dirt-stained Carhartts and t-shirt, pulled off my wool socks, and slipped into the frigid waters.

Maxine

Well, I haven't gotten very far. I'm in Albuquerque. If I'd come straight here from Frank and Alice's, it would've taken about three hours.

But my 'intuition' led me in circles and rectangles and octagons. I kept feeling these impulses to go a certain direction, but they led me nowhere. I wasn't sure which urges to follow. They made sense at the time. Alice said listen to the longings in my chest, but my chest just felt tight, the only desires I got were in my head. I've been all over the southern New Mexico countryside. *It's ridiculous!* I'll never find Sara if I can't even find my way out of New Mexico!

It was a Saturday evening and luckily no one else was hanging out at the back of the Target parking lot where I sat in the driver's seat of my minivan. My legs were sweating into the velvet-blue upholstery and I could barely keep my head up. I was done with this chase. I just wanted to hear some guidance loud and clear. *I'll go anywhere, just not going around in circles and squares in the New Mexico desert.* I'm pretty sure that's not where I'm supposed to be.

"Are you sure?" Said a voice.

It was like it was coming from my head and outside my ears all at the same time.

I ignored it. I was tired. I was at a loss for what to do next. I wanted to just head northwest but I couldn't afford to waste more money on gas. I'd saved up money for this trip, but I really didn't know how much I'd need, so I didn't want to spend it unnecessarily.

"Are you sure you were wasting time and money?"

It was more like a sound than a voice. And it kept asking stupid questions.

I shook my head, feeling a little crazy. The first tinges of cool breezed through my open windows. "Okay, whoever, whatever you are, could you at least ask me a good question if you're gonna keep this up?" Was this what the homeless people you saw talking to themselves experienced? I looked all around my van, to make sure nobody was nearby.

"What do you want for dinner?"

"A milkshake." I was glad no one was around. It felt strange and normal all at the same time to talk to this voice.

"I'll take you to a milkshake." No judgment about having a milkshake for dinner.

"I can have my GPS take me to a milkshake. I need you to take me to Sara," I answered in disgust.

"And I will," the voice responded. "But first you need to know that I'm guiding you there. You need to trust me." It wasn't a command. More like responding to something I wanted but didn't know it yet.

The cottony voice soothed and calmed me, strummed my nervous system with a joyful song. It was berries on ice cream, a pile of leaves to jump in, an icy river on a hot day. I wanted to believe the sound. But it had misled me.

"Who are you? What are you?" I moved my eyes around their sockets and kept my body still.

"Well, I'm you. I'm the non-physical part of you that's out in the Universe. Some people call me their intuition, guide, or God."

I grimaced. "I just can't tell the difference between you and my mind."

"I understand. You will. It's just a learning process like anything else. Just pay attention to when you end up where you want to be, and from trial and error, you'll get it." The sound gently continued. "You're born with it. It's just that the adults spend a lot of time telling kids they're wrong, so you eventually stop listening."

"Is that why kids seem to have so much fun and talk to themselves?" I felt foolish, but it felt good.

"Yep. Are you ready to get that milkshake?"

I grinned. "Okay, I'll try it. But I'm afraid I'm gonna mess it up again." I continued sitting straight up in the driver's seat.

"Don't worry. It's just like riding a bike. You didn't get that right the first time either."

That made so much sense!

"Now, think of the milkshake you want. Taste it, feel it on your tongue. How will that first slurp feel in your mouth?" the voice said, sounding like a hypnosis instructor.

I closed my eyes and tried to tune out the city noise. It was too hot to roll up the windows. After a few minutes of thinking about what a strawberry milkshake tastes like, I suddenly felt the berry goodness sloshing in my mouth, stinging my teeth, and making a soothing coating across my tongue and down my throat. I could smell the coldness, the redness of the berries, how plump and juicy they were when they mixed them in the shake.It made me want the shake so much more.

Is that it? I thought. *Is that how this works? I only get to THINK of the shake, not actually drink it?* I widened my eyes.

"No...." chimed in the voice, "that was just to give you a strong desire. That desire will help you hear the prompts."

"I already tried that. It didn't work! I went in circles!"

I felt insane. It was 9 pm, and I was sitting in the back of a brightly- lit parking lot talking to myself. I hoped there weren't cameras up there with those lights, otherwise the paddy wagon might drive up any minute.

"What exactly were you listening to that took you in circles? Did it sound and feel like me?"

"Nooo...." I responded, really wanting to understand. "It was more like a tension in my chest and head. It was like these two places in my chest and head were directing me." I just looked straight ahead as if the voice was on my dashboard.

"Did it feel relaxed and fun?"

My body slumped. "Of course not! I didn't know where I was going or what I was getting myself into. It was scary as shit!"

"Then that wasn't it. That wasn't your inner guidance. That's why you never got to someplace you wanted to be." The voice wasn't male or female, just sure.

I swiped back my bangs from my sweaty forehead. "Well then, what *does* it feel like? Alice said to listen to my heart and my chest is about as close to my heart as you get."

"I don't think she meant it literally." No judgment from the voice.

"Let's go back," said the voice. (Believe me, I realize how crazy it sounds that I was having a conversation with an invisible thing in the back of a Target parking lot. I just hoped no one would park beside me.) "Think of a time when you got something you really wanted. There was no effort involved, it was as if it just appeared."

"Hmm, I can't really think of anything." I wasn't exactly feeling cooperative.

"What about your friend, Trace? How did you meet?"

"Well, we just met in the cafeteria one day. We happened to be getting the same food at the same time. No big deal, it happens." This felt like a game I didn't want to play.

"And, what happened before that?" The voice ignored my attitude.

"I was in algebra class." Like the voice should know what happened.

"Had you thought about having a best friend? Is it something you asked for?"

I bit my lip and raised my eyes toward the back of my head.

"Hmm, well yeah, I guess a couple weeks earlier I was thinking about how much I'd love to have a friend to hang out with and talk about life with. I had lots of friends through the store, but none of them were gay and fatherless. None could really empathize with my life."

"And when you thought about wanting a best bud, what did you do?"

I rolled the screen back in my mind, trying to think of that time.

"OHHH!!!" When the movie got to that scene, it was like I was seeing it for the first time. "I was actually talking like I had that friend. I remember I was sitting under that gigantic maple tree on campus, feeling so lonely and lost, and I decided to just pretend that my best friend was sitting there beside me."

I beamed, so proud of myself for remembering that.

"Yes, exactly. And what else?" The voice knew.

"That's it. Whenever I thought about wanting a best friend, I just imagined what it felt like talking to her."

"Yes, exactly! You didn't dwell on it, you just moved on."

"Yeah, and your point is?" My attitude returned. I still hadn't gotten a milkshake.

"Did it feel effortful, like what you just described? Did that thinking of your best friend feel like it came from a pointed mind and a stiff chest?"

"No, it felt like a cool summer breeze just passing over my sweaty face. It was just there. Like I knew I would meet my best friend soon. Really that I already had, cuz I was already talking to her. I trusted that everything was coming together."

I was feeling humbler, understanding more of what the voice was trying to teach me.

"Perfect. Think back to how your body felt at that moment." I went back to that time. Remembering what it was like. My chest felt open. I felt like a million times myself. Not trapped in my scrawny, stick body, but like my cells reached out throughout the universe. I felt so happy and free and like I was floating down the river just being carried along and people were offering me water and food along the way. Everything just came together and I could just sit back and enjoy.

"That's it. That's the feeling! That's following your heart, your intuition, your knowing. It's like the sound of my voice. Quiet, not demanding, not like your life is going to end if you don't listen to me." The voice had gotten cheery.

My whole body softened as a smile widened my face. I took a few deep breaths and just enjoyed the quiet stillness, this moment of time, and how perfect it was. Something I really didn't think was possible in a parking lot. It was like I'd stopped listening to all the sounds around me and started listening to the sounds inside me.

"Ready to go get that shake?" the voice interrupted a few minutes later.

I sat up and nodded with a smile. When I turned the key and pulled out of the parking lot I knew where I was going even if I didn't. When I got to the first stop sign, I felt a nudge to go right. Right, I went. I drove a bit and suddenly got a nudge to go left. I couldn't safely turn then, so I went on ahead until I could turn around, then turned the way I felt guided to go.

I went down that street a couple of miles and felt another right- and there it was. *A giant neon sign with a milkshake and straw on top.* A few cars sat in the parking lot with some kids inside. It was one of those ol' timey places. All glass on top of brick. Inside three tables lined the front of the shop and there was a jukebox in the corner playing *Rock Around the Clock.*

I felt I'd found heaven itself. Not because of the milkshake, but because I'd gotten here just by listening to the nudges, just by being quiet and listening, just by KNOWING I would get here without the help of a GPS.

I sat down on the round vinyl stool, and a pink- aproned woman came over.

"What can I get for you, sweetie?" It was just like an episode of *Happy Days*.

"A large strawberry milkshake, please."

"Coming up!" She wrote on her order pad, then stuck the pencil behind her ear.

I was so proud of myself, but, I'll admit, I still wasn't convinced I could do the same to find the woman who wrote the journal.

Sara

The waters hadn't quite warmed up from the winter chill. Months without sun, takes life from the pond. The temperature hovered above the freezing mark most of the winter. I'd been swimming in that pond since I was an infant. My mema made sure I knew how to handle the water the day Mom brought me home from the hospital.

It seems odd to think that I can remember something that happened when I was so young, but I have a vivid recollection of being introduced to that cooling liquid. That time the waters had a couple months to warm up before they took me in, so it wasn't as breath sucking as the waters were now.

I'd never seen the lake water so clear.

My arms moved in a heart-shaped stroke, slowly, deliberately, trying not to disturb the water's surface and lose sight of the rock. I heard a couple of crackles come from the dense woods around the lake's edge, but I saw nothing, so I kept going. I got to the far edge of the pond, I paused and let the water go back to its clear glassiness and enjoyed the water dancing around my legs and arms as I treaded water. In water I feel like my edges melt and I can move like the most graceful of ballerinas. I go away, as my cells fuse with the water's molecules. Even in frigid waters I feel like the old is sloughing off, revealing a new shiny version of myself. Everything that mattered before becomes meaningless and I can fully enjoy life again.

After a few minutes of allowing the previous day's events to dissolve from my pores, I looked down through the lucid waters. There appeared a shimmering rock like it had been painted with diamonds and gold. But it turned out to be so much more.

I stared at the jeweled rock, feeling it was there for a reason. It was like it had been intentionally placed. I had no idea if that rock had always been there or maybe I was finally ready to see what it was hiding. *Has something in me changed that now allowed me to see it?*

I looked around at the spruce, fir, and balsamroot that was about to bloom. I felt a presence in the woods that didn't fit in. I couldn't see it, but my shoulders were tight, and I felt a knot in my stomach. I decided to ignore it, *maybe it was just the excitement of discovering this rock,* I told myself. It's never a good thing to ignore those urges.

As I continued to buoy in the water, I realized I had to make a choice. I could see what was under the rock or try to go back and fit myself in the box of the known. I took another look at the rock, and realized I had no choice. That rock was shining a light to me. Calling me to it. It was a beacon on a foggy night. What was under the rock would be the answers to all my questions. I took a deep breath as I looked at the cerulean sky, and then dove headfirst into the frigid waters and down seven feet or so.

The water was clear, but the refracting waters made it hard to get to the rock. I had to go up and take another breath. When my lungs stopped gasping for air, I heard a crunch in the forest. I looked all around and saw nothing but nature.

I should've gone to investigate. *Oh, how I wish I'd gone to look.* Something told me to stop what I was doing, but my curiosity got the best of me. Have you ever felt a nudge to do something, but you didn't, and then you ended up regretting it?

I shook my head, took another deep breath, and dove head-first into the waters with several seal kicks. This time I got to the rock, but it was slimy, and I couldn't get a grip, so back to the surface I went. As my lungs gasped for air, I felt the uneasiness in my stomach again. This was usually my sign that there was danger lurking about. But I was too excited about the rock to investigate. And like every other time I ignored that feeling, I regretted it.

I soon forgot about that feeling. I forgot about everything. I went back down and this time, before I ever touched the rock, it began to glow from the inside. I gently touched the surface. It was less like rock and more like clay. When I applied a slight pressure to the rock with my hands, it rolled off to the right, as if somebody was coming from underneath.

I had to force myself not to gasp and take in a mouthful of water. I don't know how long I hovered there looking at what I saw below. It baffled me. I hadn't known why I cared about moving that rock until I saw what it exposed. There, where moments ago there was a rock, was a dark hole!

I went back up to the surface to let my body rest and think about what to do next. But there was no denying the pull I felt to go into that hole. I didn't have a waterproof flashlight, but my instincts told me it was going to be okay. I looked all around for evidence of Brian or anyone spying on me. Nothing. I took another deep breath and dove back toward the hole.

I cautiously reached my left hand into the hole while I grasped the rock with my right. The cavity lit up like lightning bugs on a hot summer night! I quickly turned and put my feet in the shaft, smoothly sinking all the way to my knees. I felt like a moth to light. The tunnel lit up with twinkly lights, like stars in the day sky. I started floating through the air-filled shaft.

Flump! The rock rolled back over the entrance. My heart raced, and my lungs flittered. There was a conundrum between my lungs and eyes. The glowing tunnel smelled like a waterfall and wrapped me in silk sapphire sheets of space.

I floated through a shaft of star-filled air, feeling pulsed along. *Where was I going? Was I dreaming? Had the rock hit me on the head?*

A beam of light appeared beneath my feet. I was in dreamtime. *Maybe this is what people see when they die?*

Maxine

I found myself in an area where the desert meets the woods. Below was a mile of cliffs and rocks that looked like a lifeless planet. But on her rim, towering ponderosa pines and mellow green oaks ruled the scene while brown, crispy pine needles provided vital mulch for the soil who fought to keep the air from sucking her dry.

Many mornings I found circles of freshly-smashed grasses and shiny clumps of black Lima-bean sized balls, along with the tracks of elk. I especially loved it when the flattened circles were different sizes, small next to large.

Elk calves were wandering with their mamas now. They no longer had to stay hidden while Mom foraged. They were big enough to move around with her, even if a little more slowly. The elk seemed to pick the most interesting spots to sleep. When I slept outdoors, I'd find hidden corners where I couldn't be seen, always making sure I had an escape route.

But the elk slept at edges of clearings, where they could see all around them and had room to rumble if anyone came to pounce on the young.

I found myself lying down on their bedding, wanting to take in what it felt like to be them. What did it feel like to have kicking and running be your only defenses against danger? How did it feel to be hunted, when one wrong move could cost them a life? I wanted to know what it was like for them to sleep. Did they experience the stars as a blanket of love and companionship, like I did? Did they enjoy the sound of the crinkling creek below? Did the moms stay awake all night, keeping watch over the young? Or did the moms take turns sleeping?

Did they choose grassy areas over dirt-covered areas as often as they could? Did their thick hides feel the pinch of dried pine needles or the poke of a pinecone? There was so little food and water for them here, at least from what I could see, and still they thrived in the woods surrounding the Grand Canyon.

My intuition led me to a quiet spot in a crowded place. I had everything I needed for a week in Pearl. The simplicity was freeing. I loved that I could live on so little. People work hard to feel free, but is it all the stuff we buy that keeps us down?

That was something I wanted to consider as I decided what to do after my trip.

What would be the next clue in my traveling adventure? Would I find Sara?

I've been here for three days, just the trees and me. It's the first time I remember feeling so open-ended. I started living to nature's rhythm. I woke up and went to sleep with the sun. My cells expanded and my breath slowed. I spent hours looking at the tree bark, listening to the nuthatches, just noticing the smallest of flowers, and breathing the intoxicating, clear air. I've never done this before. I let the inner whispers guide me with no destination in mind. Sara's story helped me to see things in a whole new way. I didn't think it was possible to be happy just sitting on the ground, just letting thoughts pass by. I've always been rational and practical. At least until I decided to come on this trip.

But I can feel it's time to go again.

***

My last morning. The sun crept over the towering pines, and while the air still had some coolness to it, I went for a final walk to say thank you to the forest. It felt like they'd filled me with gifts the last few days, and I was just beginning to appreciate them. It would take months for me to fully understand what the riches were.

I went out to investigate the bedding of some elk who'd slept less than 100 feet from me the night before. It's been five days since I had a shower. I probably don't smell human anymore, so they didn't know to be scared.

It was unsummerly cold last night, high 30s maybe. The temperature swings in the high desert are hard to get used to. It could be 80's during the day, but freezing at night.

After cuddling in the flattened grasses, I walked back toward my camp. A white flower drew me in. Right now, wildflowers are a rare sight here. I went to see if she had a scent. Instead, she was guarding a treasure. I gently sat on the tan rocky dirt to investigate the treasure more closely. I kept my distance so as not to disturb the museum. Clinging to the bottom of the flower was a large black and white striped bumblebee! The Arnold Schwarzenegger of bees. *What kind of bee IS this?*

The sun was just beginning to light up the flower and her occupant. The bee wasn't moving at all, but somehow held tight to the underneath of the silky petals.

I sat about two feet from the flower and waited to see if the bee would move. Minutes went by and I became concerned she had frozen to death in her sleep.

Was he struck motionless as the sun moved off this spot? Or did he intentionally stop here as the lowering sun made the air colder and colder? He was in an area that would be one of the first to get the warming rays. *Was he using the daisy's face as an umbrella to protect from the evening's dew, knowing that as soon as the sun hit he'd only have to crawl a few steps to get to her pollen and shake off the cold?* What *did* bees and insects know?

I watched the bumblebee, waiting to see what story unfolded. Not so much as an antenna twitched as the air warmed. The stillness continued as the sun rose behind the trees and bathed the flower and her friend in the sun. No movement at all.

UNTIL!

I saw a twitch of his antennae, and a jolt of his front leg. One moment he was stiff as a rock, the next his legs and antennae were testing the air. I wanted to jump up and cheer but stayed at my perch, so I didn't disturb him.

He sluggishly pulled himself over the petals to the pollen, tiptoeing as he gathered breakfast. For over an hour he stayed hugging the yellow stamen of the flower, saying his prayers for making it through another night and grateful for the sweet food she was providing him in the new day. Once his belly was full, and all the cold had shivered out of his cells, he fluttered off to continue his flower dance with a different partner.

It was seeing things like this that made me wonder if I'd ever be able to go back and work a 9-5 job. There just seemed to be something greater calling me. I didn't want to run my own company, but I didn't want to be an employee either. This time in the woods, just following my instincts wherever they led, helped me dig through the years of beliefs and thoughts instilled in me by others. I realized there was so much I didn't know. It seemed like there were only a few paths to follow once we graduated from college. But I'm thinking there may be a lot more. One thing I've learned on this trip is I don't know what's around the corner, and that's okay.

Sara

The glow was coming from an opening like to the one I'd swam through at the bottom of the pond. Only this time, it was pure, like walking into a lightbulb. The light moved with sparks of green, blue and red dancing like an electrical charge. I was still floating in the speckled blue, enjoying the whirling light and wondering what to do next. *Was this it? Was this an opening?*

The light was hypnotic.

I inched the tip of my index finger toward the light. I was expecting to get shocked and prepared for the worst. But I had to know if there was more. Tentatively my fingertip reached closer and closer to the mesmerizing light. My body tensed up and I pressed my teeth on my lower lip.

I started feeling a bit of heat emanating from the white light. My body clenched more. I stopped, remembering I had been surrounded by water only moments ago. *Was my finger still wet? What was going to happen if it was?*

I brought my finger to my face and looked. It was dry. I laughed at myself. Here I was in a tunnel in the bottom of a pond, breathing air, and somehow I was still concerned about touching this light!

I took a deep breath and quickly pushed in my finger. It was like poking my finger into jello! My shoulders collapsed, and I giggled my relief. *What's happening?*

I let my finger continue moving through the gelatinous goo up to my wrist and arm-until I was up to my shoulders in a shimmering gel substance. I felt more alive than I ever had. My skin was tingling, and I couldn't stop smiling. I felt like a thousand calming feather tips and cooling slime were cradling my arms.

I recalled all the early morning swims when I knew the water was going to be 60 degrees or so. I'd learned at an early age the best thing to do was to just jump in. Somehow it was less painful than going slow.

So, I brought up my other arm, stuck it in shoulder deep and plunged in with my head. Going into anything unknown headfirst makes no sense, but nothing was making sense right then. I was certain I was either dead or dreaming.

When my whole body was inside the cloudy mix, I dolphin-kicked as much as the gel allowed, and, in only 3 kicks, I reached another opening.

As my body was suspended in the comforting jello, my head poked out the base of something that looked like a tree but moved like a ballerina. The air tingled my nose and smelled like a rain shower. I was surrounded by a live version of Monet's lily pond painting. The sky was deep blue, the tree leaves were spring green, and the pinks and purples of flowers popped like they'd been freshly oiled.

I pulled one arm out of the velvety goo, then the other and slid my body out from the tunnel and stepped down onto what felt like wet paint. Everything was fluid, yet solid. I didn't sink. I didn't float.

Immediately, a ghost-like figure appeared before me. I smiled at the rippling figure and took a deep breath. Being here reminded me of being far in the woods. It felt familiar, yet new. Like hearing my beating heart for the first time again. Yet at the same time my cells quaked.

The figure emanated serenity, and love, like meeting a Buddhist monk.

"Hi! I'm Alia. I heard you were coming." Her deep blue eyes looked like two swimming pools at the plushest of resorts. Her body was rippling ribbons of light, no limbs the same, every surface curved and jovial.

My stomach quivered, but my heart opened, and a smile covered my face. I shook my head, "How were you told I was coming when I don't know where I am?" I felt wobbly, not sure if I could stand.

"You're here! That's where you are." She beamed. Her voice reminded me of the sound the trees make. It's resonant, and soothing, like the lightest of breeze kissing my cheeks.

My nervous system was alight, trying to figure out what neurons to fire; happy, fearful, sad? "Am I dead? Why do I feel like I'm in a dream?"

"Welcome to Ilanaly," she responded, ignoring my question. I looked all around."Ilanaly. Where is this? Underground?" I'd been finding my way around the woods without a GPS for decades. It was unnerving to not have any idea where I was-or even which way was up.

"Noooo." She almost sang. "The way people are digging into the ground and exploding things we'd been goners a long time ago. We're somewhere else." I felt like I'd swum into a Dr. Seuss story. She didn't really answer my questions, just created more.

I turned away from Alia. I couldn't take that conversation. My brain couldn't process thoughts and questions. It had become mush, like the surroundings.

Alia reached out her hand. "Come, let me introduce you to some others. They'll be so happy you're here!" Her voice was like a nun's, quiet yet expressive.

We glopped, feeling like we were walking on several feet of wet paint. Occasionally, another airy figure would float by. Everyone seemed to know me, even though I didn't even know where I was. *I MUST be dreaming.* "Nope, you're not dreaming. We're as real as your family on earth," Alia responded.

I was wondering if it was a good idea to go with this person and at the same time, feeling pretty certain I couldn't get back to the farm even if I wanted to. "You can hear my thoughts?" I stopped. "That seems kinda rude-to read my thoughts." Wherever I was, felt like it *was* me. Like my cells had expanded and morphed and created a whole world.

Alia turned around, still smiling, "Well, only if you have something to hide. Here, we find it much easier than using our mouths. No judgment, so nothing to hide." She shrugged her shoulders like reading someone's mind was the most normal thing in the world.

"Nothing to hide? Who has nothing to hide? What if you don't like someone?"

"Well, that's okay, you don't have to like everyone. Why would you?" Alia tried to keep going, but my questions were thwarting her progress.

With a sigh, I continued to follow her. *Crap! This reading my thoughts thing was going to get some getting used to.*

"Oh, you'll catch on in no time. It's much simpler." Alia was once again responding to my thoughts. "You know you already do it with the animals and trees you talk to on earth." She tried to look into my eyes, but her eyes were like lasers. It was freaky, like they were cutting open my brain.

"How do you know about that?" I said out loud.

"I have connections." She started glowing! She seemed quite pleased with herself, as if she'd told a joke.

I laughed. As much as I wanted to be scared, I couldn't.

The painted ground changed colors as we moved across. Ahead of us were tree-like figures with green, orange and reds pulsing through their bodies, while the branches displayed waves of yellow that broke out to purple toned leaves.

The water flowed in rivulets of its own choosing. No ground would hold it down. It circled above our heads, around our bodies, and even across the white sky.

I saw a figure reach up with his hands and grasp some of the water and bring it to his mouth. The water was about the only thing that was the color I thought it should be. Everything else just seemed to be random.

"It's not random. You're making up the colors. I see different things than you," Alia responding to my thoughts again. "You see lots of trees and figures that look like people because that's what you know. What I see is more of what you'd call abstract."

"How can I be making this up? I thought this was all a dream." I wanted to collapse. I was exhausted. My brain just couldn't comprehend what was happening.

"No, a dream happens when you're asleep, and right now you're more awake than you've probably ever been," Alia said with her thoughts, not her mouth.

"Oh crap, that mind thing again," I said out loud.

"You'll get used to it."

I continued to need to say things out loud. "So you're not the shape I see, which is kind of like a girl with flowing hair?"

She just smiled at me. "Nope, that's all you."

"It can't be me. I see you so clearly." I shook my head.

"Do you know what a hologram is?"

"Well, I've read about them, but I've never seen one."

Alia's arms started waving through the air. "A hologram is a projection, right? Something someone created with multiple images and light refraction then projected it into the air. Well, here your brain is the artist, and it's projecting your thoughts and beliefs!" She twirled around and lept all in one fluid motion that rivaled the greatest of dancers.

"There's no way I could make this up! I'm not that creative."

"Why do you say that?" Alia's nose crinkled and her head tipped to one side as she actually spoke the words.

"You're talking to the girl who flunked art."

"Flunked art? How does someone else determine what's art? That's crazy." She looked at me like she genuinely didn't know how that was possible.

"Well, it's how it is on earth." Wanting to change the subject, I asked, "can you see what I see?"

"I could if I wanted to, but I have no need to." She said matter-of-factly.

"Oh *good*, something private." I sneered.

Alia smiled. Or maybe that's just what I projected she did.

We continued to glide towards a group of people picking fruit and tending to a garden. Well, that's what I saw, anyway. Who knows what they were doing. It was peaceful and quiet with just a hint of breeze. The place was filled with light, but I didn't see a sun. This felt like where my cells were born, and everything around was part of my DNA.

"Sara," one of the group yelled, "it's so good to have you here! We're so excited to meet you." It was weird that people I'd never met knew my name and seemed more excited to see me than my own family.

Alia introduced them. The orange woman was Tansy, the mauve man was Stance, the yellow woman was Morna, and the little girl was Shan.

If I was making this up, why was I seeing things in such odd colors?

A giggle rose from my belly, tickled my throat and overtook my body. I fell to the ground, overflowing with uncontrollable laughter. My breath came in short bursts between the tummy quakes. Years of restraint unrolled up my throat and over my tongue. The squishy ground cradled me as everyone looked at me with grinning eyes. "Oh, that felt so good. I just met you people and here I feel like myself, like you get me, you know me without judgment. Why is that? How can it be that it feels so good to be here? Where am I?"

They just looked at each other and smiled.

"Come, let's go introduce you to some others. They'll be so happy you're finally here," said Alia, reaching for my hand.

Finally, here? It's sounding more and more like I died.

Alia responded, "Sara, you haven't died, you're just in the original world."

I shook my head. "Did you say this is the original world? What does that mean?"

Shan squeezed my hand.

Maxine

You won't believe what just happened. I still can't believe it! I want to shout about it from the rooftops. I want to call everyone I know. And yet, there's a part of me that just wants to keep it all to myself for fear that others will belittle the miraculous moment. I want the awe to sink into my cells and permanently attach to my neural pathways, as a reminder of what's possible, what can happen when I follow my intuition.

So I was driving down this beautiful canyon in central Oregon. The place I wanted to spend the night was all snowed in. Even finding out about that place was serendipitous, but I'll tell you about that later. This miracle I just witnessed, I have to get it down, to know it's real, to hear myself talk about it, to feel the fullness of the moment.

It was getting dusk. I was concerned about finding a place to camp for the night.

I suddenly got this urge to turn left. I couldn't stop that fast, so I pulled over into a turnout a few hundred feet down the road. The road I felt an urge to turn left onto seemed big and well used. It was one that campers and regular cars could navigate, so I wasn't that interested in it. But to the right of the turnout was a small forest service road that went almost straight up. There was no sign of traffic on it, so I tried it out instead. I still didn't always trust my urges. There was still a part of me that believed that logic ruled. Well, of course, you know what happened. After driving for a couple of miles, I couldn't find a place to camp. Worse, a shady-looking guy passed me going down, and I didn't feel good with him knowing I might camp out there by myself. People ask me how I feel safe and that's really it. I just have to follow my gut. I never know what doesn't happen.

The 'wrong turns' I'd taken that led me to blissful places were made because they didn't give me the luxury of thinking things through. Sara's notebook made me aware of this. So I turned around and went up the gravel drive that I felt drawn to initially. I drove the tree-tunnel road a couple of miles until I felt the urge to go down a minor road to the left. I went down the path about 50 feet, it was barely passable by my Pearl, so I stopped in the middle of the unused lane.

I got out and took in the sedate summer air. I walked down toward the end of the lane to see if there was going to be any way to turn around. The lush canyon allowed as much vegetation to grow in the middle of the road as on the sides. About 500 feet from where I left Pearl I came upon a little clearing on the left side of the lane, and there, standing before me, was the reason I was certain I was called down this path. Towering above everything was a mammoth Douglas fir and his big leaf maple companion. I didn't think I had enough friends to encircle the fir tree because she was so big. The maple's leaves were verdant green, having only been out for a few weeks. They danced together in the violet filled forest. A dribbling stream fed their feet. The fir's branches didn't start until much higher than the Maple's. But when their arms met, they entwined and cuddled each other, creating an iridescent green canopy for the violets, grasses and vanilla leaf wildflowers below.

This entire area had been thoroughly logged decades ago, but these two beauties had been spared. They were growing old together. My eyes welled up. The sun glowed between the surrounding slender tree trunks to the west, being allowed to barely show itself. It felt like a fairy world, and I was an invading giant. It was the most beautiful spot I'd ever seen, and I was just guided there. There was no map to get me there, and it looked like the road was rarely used. No sign of discarded trash or toilet paper, no abandoned campfires. Just an old logging road where the plants were winning the land battle.

I pulled Pearl into a little nook the gravel made. I have a rule-I don't drive on plants. How would I feel if someone drove on my home or in my yard? I leave as few marks as possible. I'm only here getting to care for this land. It's a gift given to each of us, and it's my job to take good care of that gift-and not smash it with my tires. I'm not sure how I came to this. It wasn't something I was taught. But I knew with every cell of being that the forest and her inhabitants were created by God as a reminder of what was really important.

But you know what? I haven't even gotten to the miracle yet!

I slept in Pearl that night so as not to interfere with this dream land any more than I had.The fir and maple were my guardian angels. All night, they stood as sentinels, reaching to the sky-and almost making it. Their presence mothered me and allowed me a deep sleep.

When the first rays of light showed the tree's contours I started wondering... *What had they seen? Had they been here before my ancestors landed on the shores of this continent?*

While I sipped my morning tea, I strolled down the hidden road. I had only gotten about half a mile when sadness took over my reverie. There, on the side of the gravel was the fresh, lifeless body of a chipmunk.

I quickly kneeled next to the body and examined him with my eyes. There was no sign of trauma. I gently wrapped my fingers around his still plump tummy so I could move him into the brush and give him a safe resting place. Suddenly his belly expanded in a tired breath. My skin lept.

It was a chilly morning, so once I recovered, I laid his little body in a sunny spot to see if warmth would give him life. I left him alone as I continued my walk through the low bright green leaf tunnel saying prayers for the striped beauty.

When I got back to the spot, his eyes were still closed, but his once sporadic breathing was more regular. I shivered wondering if I had helped bring this woodland creature back from the brink. I gently cradled him in my palms as I carried him to my camp. As I inched along the last quarter mile, I allowed the pulsing sensation of love to flow through my hands and into his body. Sara's words from the notebook were igniting my cells and teaching them new things.

My empty beach chair made a recovery room in case any dogs or other danger came tromping down the road. I walked away to give him unthreatened space. Ever think you're having a great idea, and it turns out to be the completely wrong thing to do?

Minutes later I glanced his way and caught him trying to crawl off my chair even though his eyes were still closed. He plopped onto the ground before I could rescue him. I scooped him up again and found another sunny spot, worried he may have injured himself again. This time I made him a healing space on the ground surrounded by a towel. I should've found a better spot.

As soon as I returned to my watching post, I heard a dreaded sound. The jingling of a dog collar. Worse, it was two, not one! I jumped up and yelled, "Please restrain your dogs." But there were no humans in sight. The dogs kept galloping toward me and I yelled for them to stop.

It was two huskies just out for their morning run and didn't care about me or my commands.

I yelled again. "Please call your dogs!" No response. Still no humans in sight. They got closer and closer to the recovering chipmunk. I didn't know if I could get to him before the dogs did. I kept trying to wave off the dogs, while running towards the ailing body. *Please, please, please don't let them get to the chipmunk!* I pleaded. I felt so stupid for sitting so far away, for not being closer and protecting him. Something had told me some dogs would come, and I was kicking myself for not listening.

The dogs were galloping happily, totally unaware of my fears and concerns, just out for play. I didn't know how huskies felt about little chipmunk bodies and I didn't want to find out. I ran as hard as I could, as they started closing in, closer, closer, closer....

No please, please no!

Suddenly, they stopped.

We all stood still. I watched them for the slightest movement. As their tongues hung low and their gray-white sides heaved, they looked at each other then turned back the way they came. Something had gotten their attention. I was just glad it wasn't the chipmunk.

I took a deep breath, brushed the hair out of my eyes and looked toward the chipmunk. My fear turned upside down. He was crawling around! His eyes were still closed, but he was sniffing the ground like a chipmunk does when looking for food! I wanted to give him water, but I had read that ailing wildlife can easily drown if not given just droplets of water while they recover, so, instead, I crushed up some raw almonds and pecans and sprinkled them on the surrounding ground.

Other chipmunks came to check out the goods. The once lifeless chipmunk moved slowly as two others skittered around.

Then suddenly he slumped over and it wiped the smile from my face.

NOOOO!! He was doing so well.

I kept some distance and visualized streams of love pouring into his body. I just imagined his whole body being filled with life and love and willing, whatever was ailing him, to be repaired.

I held my breath, waiting, hoping, believing he'd be alright. The seconds crawled by like a snail. I had to keep reminding myself to breathe. I debated whether to pick him up or leave him there. I kept rethinking my decisions, maybe if I'd.....

Then, after what seemed to be an eternity, he suddenly sat up in his chipmunk way and chomped on a bit of nut. His eyes glimmered, and he looked just like his buddies! He ate some more morsels and a moment later he BOUNDED into the bushes!

I gasped as my cells shivered. I could hardly retain my joy. This lifeless body I'd just found maybe 60 minutes before was now looking like a happy chipmunk going on his way. He didn't pause to say thanks; he was just gone.

I stared at the spot where he'd been lying helpless, just to be sure he was actually gone. I kept an eye on the bushes he'd bounded into, looking for signs of him. There were several chipmunks skittering around now, sniffing out the bits of nut I'd left. I'd never been so happy to not be able to tell them apart.

I took a deep breath as the tears rolled down my face. I sprung up and boogied about, overwhelmed with joy and gratitude. I didn't feel I'd done anything except see the chipmunk healed. I wondered if I could do this with people.

People who weren't there may never be able to understand the miracle of it all, they may say he was just sleeping. But they didn't see the labored breaths or his inability to open his eyes, or the way he dragged his body along the ground. I witnessed a miracle. And I know it won't be the last.

$\mathcal{S}ara$

I slowly adapted to life in Ilanaly. I came to enjoy the quiet that mind-reading allowed. I had found my people, my community, something I'd never felt on earth. Being there was like being in the woods, just love and kindness, no judgment, nobody's baggage. Everyone took responsibility for their lives.

The people of Ilanaly taught me so much. They said I had these abilities all along. That most people do, but our human brains keep us from expressing them. Some people want to control others, but when we all know how powerful we are, then no one is in control of us. No one ever is.

It wasn't only the trees that talked, now I could ask the waters to move, the animals to help, and I could do anything I could see in my mind. If I could dream it, I could do it. Including flying! Some people would put their hands on the trees or water to hear what they were saying. Some people, like me, could just hear them. Some people were more visual or feeling oriented in the way they connected with others.

In Ilanaly, everything worked together. The plants communicated with each other. A network, much like what I imagined our brain's neural pathways looked like, ran through the ground. The people treated the animals, plants and land as if they were beloved children. And in return, they were easily provided with everything they needed. The more I relaxed, the less I saw things as they were on earth and started just seeing shapes of shimmering color.

The sky appeared to me as glowing swirls of white and blue. As far as I could see there were floating dots of yellow, orange and red reminding me of stemless wildflowers. Often it looked like a giant paintbrush was creating them as I looked on. I never saw what the source of light was. It was like everything had its own inner light that glowed to contribute to the daylight. It went out for 10 hours every night. I liked the mystery of it all and making new discoveries each day, so I never asked where the light came from. I hadn't felt any anger or hatred from anyone here. My edges melted, my breath slowed, and I moved to the rhythm of a heartbeat. We slept in an open field on a mesa about 20 feet above the gathering space. I never saw any homes or buildings. We just laid down on the cushioned moss which sprung back each morning.

We ate meals in the park-like area that was at the center of everything I saw. Tables were covered with colorful swimming clothes, and everyone sat on invisible chairs. The meals felt more like an opportunity to gather than to replenish lost energy. I never saw anyone cooking, but these buffets always appeared. At each gathering there was a smorgasbord of food. There were cooked meats and raw veggies and the deepest blue blueberries I'd ever seen. It shocked me to see foods that were so familiar. But the taste! The taste was more than anything I'd ever experienced. This wasn't grocery store stuff. I'd never even tasted blueberries this good from our wild bushes. These were the blueberries I dreamed of! They were plump and juicy, and filled with that subtle sweetness that I love blueberries for.

There didn't seem to be any order. Everyone moved to an inner rhythm. They gardened for the joy of it, and washed clothes in laughter-filled groups. I couldn't see that anything was being made, but they had everything they needed. It seemed things just appeared. I tried to ask about it, but they just squeezed my hand. I would find out when the time was right.

And I met Joel. Joel may be the first man I've loved. Definitely the first man that I felt saw and appreciated all of me. There was no judgment when he looked at me. He loved my human failings. I had a soft place to fall. I was drenched in care and understanding, and I didn't feel alone anymore.

We met the day I arrived, and it was like we were meant to be together. We spent hours walking. He showed me around Ilanaly, though he said this was just a welcoming place. Ilanaly was endless and I'd get to know more of this world when the time was right.

I'd never enjoyed just being with someone so much. It didn't matter if we talked or did anything. I just loved hanging out with him. There was a familiarity that I'd only ever felt with trees. He was slightly taller than me and I saw him as a cross of Bruce Springstein's roughness and John Lennon's kindness. He smelled like the earth that I had slept on so many times around Washington state.

But there was a glitch. Joel couldn't live on Earth. He couldn't breathe the air there for long. His body would start to shut down. I didn't know if I could stay in Ilanaly. I felt an urge to help people know what I knew about the trees. For people to know the wisdom that pulsed through their trunks and leaves. To realize they were life for us. That diversity of size and species of plants was important for all life, not just their own.

So as perfect as the days were, literally flowing one into the next, Joel knew the thread connecting me to Earth relentlessly tugged at me.

"I just want to be happy, Joel, and I can't imagine being happier than this," I said one day while we were floating on the stream's clear surface.

"Sara, everything has a reason. You weren't born here for a reason. You have a purpose on Earth." Joel's voice was a breeze floating through the pine trees. I could listen to him read the constitution and it would mesmerize me.

I stopped mid-stride and turned toward Joel. "But what about us? I don't want to live without you anymore."

"Without me?" Joel laughed. "I'll be supporting you from here. You won't be on your own. You never were." He gathered me into his arms and held me gently.

I wished I'd enjoyed our time together more instead of fretting about the future. If I'd known what was coming, or rather *who* was coming, I wouldn't have wasted a moment of my time with Joel.

Maxine

Sprinkled in the sun-filled air are little bits of gray particles floating on the summer winds. The color of the sky is an orangey red, as the sun's light reflects off the ash particles. My lungs have to filter the ash. There's no filtering the smell though.

At a diner near Moab Utah, I heard some fellas talking about the beginning of fire season. Summer brings careless campers who have campfires even when the signs say not to, and worse, they leave warm coals. People have this false idea that if there's no fire showing, then they've put it out. But in the high winds that plague California and the mountain Southwest in June and July, those warm coals are fanned to life then jump into the nearby brittle vegetation. This is how massive wildfires begin, killing wildlife, life-giving trees and burning down people's homes.

I often wonder if those who can't be bothered to completely put out their campfires feel any guilt about the death they've created. It's the same with those who leave their trash in the woods for others to pick up. How do they sleep at night?

Every time I hear of these human-caused disasters, I feel a pain in my chest. But this time, it gave me guidance. A wildfire, would Sara be there?

Outside the diner, I sat in Pearl, looking at my road atlas, figuring out the best route to get to where there were enormous fires. I was attentive to how things felt in my body as I contemplated each road and places to sleep on the two-day journey.

I still felt like an idiot. *Was that a good feeling about driving I 80 or was I just excited that it meant I could stop at a Trader Joe's? Did I not want to go by that back country road because I was scared of being so far from civilization and something happening I couldn't get out of?* These were some thoughts that rambled around my brain as I tried to determine a way forward. The pathways in my brain felt like a wire that had come loose from an electric pole, sizzling, sparking, flashing around, and just looking for a place to go. More energy moved around my brain than I had places to direct it. I felt exhausted.

This following your intuition can be hard! I thought it was supposed to be easy!

"It is. It's like everything. The more you do, the easier it gets." I hadn't heard the voice in some time. I'd been just following interior prompts.

The sound seemed to just pop up at random times. When I felt like I could really use her guidance, nothing, *nada*, not so much as a water drop of information. But then when I'd given up believing that she'll ever say anything again, up she pops with words I'm sure are helpful, but sometimes they feel more infuriating.

"Thanks, I'm working on it." I replied. "It can be exasperating. It feels like it'd be so much easier to just take the fastest route." I wanted to follow the invisible path, but sometimes I questioned if it really existed. Who was I to be given such guidance?

"You can do whatever you want. It's always your choice," she continued, saying things that had no practical application. "I know...." I put my head in my hand.

I looked at the map again. This one route just kept popping out at me. It was so roundabout, going all the way around to the other side of the fire. It seemed crazy. I didn't have an endless supply of gas money- but I was committed to following my intuition. She'd taken me to some beautiful spots and connected me with great people in the last couple of weeks. So I folded my map back so I could follow the route. Pearl purred to a start. I pulled out of the diner parking lot and headed towards the Sierra Nevada Mountains near Lake Tahoe.

Sara

Joel and I were sitting by the emerald falls, having a picnic. All the days in Ilanaly were lovely. It rained, but just enough every few days. The temperature was always comfortable for a long-sleeved shirt, and I didn't have to wear a hat.

What was interesting was that it seemed I had totally changed my wardrobe. I wore dresses and skirts and flowing pants rather than the carhartts and denim shirts which had been the uniform for my whole life. There just seemed to be something that lent itself to a more fluid way of dressing. I felt free. I danced and floated everywhere.

And with Joel I felt like an equal. He wasn't like most men I'd met where I felt the need to show that I was just as strong and capable as they were. With Joel, there was no question.

My mind had been as quiet as a baby's room and laughter filled my lungs. The bluebells were serenading us, as I laid in the grass with my eyes closed and feeling every cell filled with joy and gratitude. I didn't think it was possible to break my sense of peace. Boy was I wrong.

"Well, isn't this a pretty place? Don't think I've ever seen you in a dress."

My heart about pounded out of my chest and my whole body stiffened. *It had to be a dream.* I had to be sleeping. I didn't want to open my eyes. I wanted it to be my imagination. That voice couldn't belong to who I feared it did, could it?

"What? I came all this way and you're not even going to say hello?"

I couldn't deny it, it was him. *How....how...?*

I took a deep breath, sat up and looked at Joel. He looked at me with his child-like grin like nothing had changed. I didn't want to move my eyes from that place, the moment I did, everything would change. I'd have to acknowledge the truth of the situation, and every cell fought to keep that from happening. But I had no choice.

I looked up, and my greatest fear loomed over me.

Brian.

I just stared, my heart beating faster and faster. Joel laid his hand on mine.

"Hi, Brian, I'm Joel." Joel greeted him like it was the most natural thing in the world that he was here.

"How the hell do you know who I am?" Brian replied, always so pleasant.

"I just do." Joel smiled back.

"Brian, how did you get here?" I squeaked out.

"With my friend Bulldozer." He grinned, so proud of himself. "I saw you that day. But I couldn't move that rock." He pointed up toward the cave entrance. "Had to drain the pond so I could get a bulldozer to move it. I didn't realize how strong you were."

"I don't understand, how'd you get through the tunnel?" I stammered.

"Oh, I practically had to chisel my way through that thing. Wondered if I could make it bigger so more people could go through." Brian gloated.

I just wanted him to be gone. This pristine place, this perfection, now had a dark being running through it. Nothing good could come from Brian's presence here. It never did.

"You were gonna keep this all to yourself weren't ya, Sis?" Brian continued, like we had invited him. "Just like you not to share, not to tell me about this treasure you found." He stared straight at me.

"Well, you always broke whatever toys I had...." I took his bait. "....whatever good I had, so it's better to keep these things to myself."

"Ah come on, Sis. There's a gold mine here. We could make millions selling tickets to this place. And since you got me fired, it's the least you can do." Brian swung his arms to encompass everything around us.

I bolted upright and faced the thing that caused terror within me.

Everyone always said how brave I was. They'd not seen me with Brian.

"Brian, you will not sell tickets to this place. It's not yours to sell!" I stood nose-to-nose with my least favorite person. Someone I'd loved and admired as a little girl. But that was before he changed.

"Well, access to it is on my property, so I can do what I want." He snickered.

"No, Brian," I retaliated, "you don't own the farm, not one speck of it! Mom owns it and when she dies, it ALL goes to me. Mom knows all you care about is how much money you can make, not protecting what Mema and Grandad created." I was working hard to keep my fear hidden.

"You guys are so stupid. With the money you could make off this place, you could buy a hundred farms." Brian shook his head.

"I don't want a hundred. I want the one we have." My voice dropped, thinking of our beautiful land.

"Well, you're here, and Mom sure as hell won't stop me from setting up shop around the hole to here. We'll call it Alice's Wonderland!" His hand swept across the sky like there was some enormous banner there. "Isn't that great!? Get it? Just like Alice going through the bunny hole. OR maybe after you, dear Sis, I should call it Sara's Wonderland, that way you can make some money off your name. I wouldn't leave you empty-handed."

I felt like flames were coming off the top of my head. Joel wrapped his arm around me and squeezed gently as if to tell me it was gonna be alright. But he didn't know Brian. He didn't know the destruction that man-child was capable of. I wasn't sure what Joel knew of hatred and pain. He'd lived in paradise his whole life.

"Brian, you're gonna have a huge fight on your hands," I said confidently.

"Oh, I'm counting on it, little Sis. I'd love to see what you can do to stop me. You know Mom, she doesn't want to get me riled up. I think she's a little afraid of me." The smirk on his face was a familiar one, one that meant that what was to come was going to make Mom cry.

It also meant me backing down so as not to get Mom upset. That's how it had always been.

But not this time.

"Well, I'll let you two lovebirds get back to your pondering all this beauty." Brian's eyes glimmered. "Enjoy the quiet as long as you can. I think tickets to this place are gonna sell out really fast." He laughed as he looked around. "AND it looks like there's gold in that stream. I've got some prospecting friends who'll pay dearly to get some of that."

I lunged toward Brian to tackle him, but Joel held me back and whispered, "it's okay, it's going to be okay."

I sneered at Brian. He just laughed back.

"See ya', Sis! We'll be back!" He sauntered off, laughing the whole way.

I collapsed, and my body shook with uncontrollable sobs. "Joel, what are we going to do? There's no way this will be okay. You don't know Brian. You don't know what he's capable of. This is a man who would trap squirrels and skin them alive while they hung upside down by their tails, just so he could sell tickets of the skinning to his friends. He'll stop at nothing to make a few bucks." I was glad Joel could read my mind, as I didn't have the energy to form the words with my lips.

"Honey, Sara, I know. I've been told. The animals have told us the horror stories about what he's done. We know what goes on up there. That he only cares about fancy cars and clothes. But we have Ilanaly on our side. There's a reason it took him so long to get in. That rock was working hard to keep him out. But maybe this was a catalyst, maybe he ultimately was supposed to get in."

"But he got in using a bulldozer and draining the pond! He will go to even bigger lengths to get his way. I can't stay here, Joel. I've got to go back there and do everything I can to keep him off Mom's property. She doesn't have the strength." I sat up and looked into Joel's eyes.

"And maybe, this was the Universe's way of telling you it's time for you to go back." Joel wrapped his arms around me and kissed my hair several times. "We will get through this, Sara. There's more to this than I can tell you right now."

The tears just kept coming. I didn't want to leave. Especially Joel. But since he couldn't breathe on earth, I had to go fight this thing alone.

Maxine

Crap! They won't let me anywhere near the fire!! Why the hell did I come this way! Sara surely isn't way out here.

I'd followed my guidance to the back side of the fire. The wind was fanning the flames and smoke toward Nevada, so at least I was safe here. As much as a part of me wanted to get here as fast as I could, I kept feeling these tugs to stop and hike and enjoy the drive.

I'm glad I did. I hiked in wildflower filled meadows and tromped through tenacious snow that was refusing to melt and head down the mountains. I saw more animal tracks than human ones. At night I saw stars I'd never seen before. The Utah sky is so clear, it's like you can pluck the stars out of the sky and go for a ride.

But what now?

I sat in a pullout on a gravel road overlooking the camp where all the firefighters slept and ate. I'd been watching them for about an hour. A green truck pulled up near the tents, and out stumbled the soot covered heroes of the wild. They willed their legs to walk to their tent. Their eyes were weary and sad.

I imagined the things they must see out there, things that never make the nightly news. The corpse of burned bears and fawns. Antlers being the only thing left of an elderly elk that survived everything but human ignorance. I wondered what the firefighters experienced, but was also afraid to know.

I feel like I'm supposed to walk over to that camp, but I'm scared shitless. *What if they know I'm an imposter?* There's no way they won't unless I go roll in the dirt somewhere. Even though I haven't showered in two days, I'm glistening clean compared to those people.

So right now, I'm just staring, trying to get myself to just open the door, or drive closer to the camp. There isn't much activity right now. They're probably sleeping or working. I'm so far away from the fire, I can't even hear the helicopters or airplanes. *What could I possibly say to these people?*

The inner nudge ignored my pleas and became stronger than my fear. I slipped on my Keen sandals and walked forward with a pace normally reserved for getting away from danger. If I slowed down, I was afraid my mind would take over and hold me back.

The smell of smoke pervaded the camp. Even this far away, they brought their work with them. The dusty dirt field was surrounded by dead grasses and out-houses. The tents were in rainbowed rows.

I sat at the edge of the colorful display and waited until I knew what I was doing there.

I sat and sat and sat and sat then the sun started its downward journey. A million times in the last few hours, I wanted to get up and leave, but something kept me here, kept me anchored to the dust.

"Hi, I've seen you sittin here most of the day. Something I can do for you?"

I guess I'd nodded off. My head jerked, and I covered my eyes from the glare as I looked up at the person standing over me. It was a slender, muscled young woman in a tank top and shorts. Her bark-colored hair was pulled back in a ponytail with many strands successfully escaping the rubber band. She glowed like there was an inner sun in her.

I tried to jump up, but it looked more like a baby giraffe's first attempt to rise.

"Hi, I'....m sorry. I'm not sure why I'm here...... I just felt like I was supposed to come," I stammered. I hung my head. I couldn't believe I'd said that out loud. *Now she's really gonna think I'm a nut and call the police.*

"Ah, well, that's fine." Her disheveled teeth showed under her lips. She reached out to shake my hand. I'm Molly. I don't go back out until tomorrow, so let me know if I can help."

I stood staring into her eyes, shaking her hand. Feeling like I was supposed to say something.

"Want a cold drink?" That's all I could muster. I shook my head. I'm sure they're provided with food and drinks.

Molly giggled. "Sure, what do you have? .....getting tired of the same ole things they serve us here."

Then I realized how little I had to offer. "Ginger ale? Seltzer water?"

"Umm, ginger ale would be great! Where ya' stashing this stuff?" Molly looked around.

"Oh! My car is over there." I pointed to the forest road where Pearl was parked. "I can go get it and bring it here."

"Not at all. I'll walk there with you." Molly started toward the van.

She chatted away, wondering where I was from, what I did, how I found this place. As I tried to keep up with her questions, and wondering how much detail she wanted, I noticed how relaxed I felt. Our nimble, easy steps wandered down the newly-formed trail. The breeze provided welcome relief from the heat.

I slid open the door, popped open the cooler and handed Molly a drink. We continued talking about this and that. It turned out we were the same age. Molly had become a fire-fighter during her second year of college summer break and loved it so much she just kept coming back. She wasn't at all offended when I asked her about being a woman in a man dominated world.

"It's true, but these are good guys. As long as I can do the work and keep up, they're good. No special treatment. We're here to save lives."

Then I asked her about Sara. I don't know why, it just blurted out of my mouth.

"How do you know her?" Molly's eyebrows creased as she stepped back and pierced her eyes into mine.

"I don't." I fumbled, sorry I'd asked. "I found a notebook she left in New Mexico, and I just want to find her."

"Oh." She waved her hand in the air, turned and walked off. Not so much as a goodbye.

The sun had lowered, and the only sound was the gurgling creek nearby. The quaking trees reminded me of how alone I felt.

I thought we had a connection. What happened? I watched Molly jog back to her tent as if we'd never met and disappear. My feet were cemented to the ground but my heart wanted to find her again.

Moments went by as I stared into the empty space wishing I had someone to talk this event through with. If I was home, I'd have ready counsel, but out here, I just had air. I forced back my tears, slid into Pearl's front seat, turned the ignition key and headed up the hill behind me for the night.

***

I drove about a mile up a pot-hole filled road until I found a place to camp for the night. I wasn't in the mood to follow my intuition, I just wanted to curl up in a ball and go to sleep. I laid on the hood of my minivan under the bright starlight, feeling empty and purposeless. There's nothing like the dense stillness to leave you naked with your thoughts. You can't tuck them behind the stars, you can't turn on the TV and drown them out. They're just there. I wanted a drink, anything to make the pain go away. But I only had books and I just couldn't read right now.

'I suck at this.' I thought to myself. *What had I said? Why had Molly run off like that?* Over and over again, our conversation ran through my head. The merry-go-round exhausted me, but sleep didn't come.

I sunk myself into the glistening stars, trying to feel I wasn't alone.

Only moments had passed when the dreaded thump, thump, thump of someone's bass came oozing out of their car speakers in the distance. *No!* I thought, *please don't let them be coming up here.* People aren't aware of how much their music and voices carry through the trees and air currents. I looked over my shoulder and saw the stealy headlights winding up the road, the thumping getting louder and louder. The headlights stopped about ¼ mile from me. I shuddered.

The once quiet air became filled with laughing ripe voices, yelling, ever loudening music drowning out the night and headlights left on to brighten their spot. At least they didn't start a fire, but the peace was gone. I waited about 20 minutes to see if they'd move on.

"Please turn down your music!" Mom had ingrained such politeness in me that I couldn't even insist without being nice. But I doubted they could hear me.

These kids didn't care. They didn't come to the woods for quiet, they came to get away from authority, like so many do. It doesn't occur to them that rules are made for people who aren't considerate of those around them. They only care about what they want, so laws and rules have to be made to ensure the rights of others.

I threw my pad and bag in the back of Pearl, slammed the door shut and stomped on the gas. *Nothing pisses me off more than inconsiderate people.* People who are so wrapped up in their rights that they don't stop to consider the rights of others.

I sped down the forest service road. They would fill this valley with their screams and pounding noise all the way to the top. With no buildings to stop it, sound carries effortlessly up the valley curves.

I didn't know where I was going. I just wanted to get away from there.

I got down to the main road and turned right, then slowly eased my way up the paved road until I came to another forest service road that crossed a creek. All I could see were the trees as they jumped into my headlights, and a gravel road in front of me. I eased my way up north, away from the partiers. Driving at night always feels like I've driven for hours. I don't know how far I went. My windows were down, the cool night air filled my nostrils, and the chirping grasshoppers filled my eardrums.

I was so deep in thought, so lost in my musings, that I almost didn't feel the voice yelling at me to stop. I slammed on my brakes and Pearl slid to a stop. There, staring at me, was a bobcat and kit. They were as surprised by me as I was by them. The kit sat down 10 feet in front of me and looked around while the mom continued to pierce my windshield with her questioning eyes. There was nothing there, no malice, no judgment, no "watch where you're going" just "what should I do now? Is it safe?" Meanwhile, the kit explored the road lit by my headlights, totally unaware of the killing machine that was before him. I loved his innocence. I think that's one reason people like children so much. They haven't become filled with fear yet. In their world, everything is a toy and life is for exploration. Mom Bobcat and I pondered each other for a few minutes, then the kit found a grasshopper to play with and pounced. Mom shook her head and leapt to the other side of the road, but the kit seemed to not even know I was there. She scratched on a log, jumped around some rocks, and playfully followed her mom, who'd walked into the dark.

My heart pounded as I finally took a breath and smiled. "Thank you," I whispered to the air, "thank you." I was complete. I felt like I knew why I'd been pushed by the partiers to come this way. A theme I'd been noticing on this trip is when I'm pushed off my mountaintop, I'm led to a paradise. Just when I think it can't get better. It does.

Seeing a wild animal just going about their life, living the way they were meant, reminded me of my roots, who I truly am, my naturalness. There's nothing quite like the beauty of a wild animal at home in his world. They're untamed and unimpressed by humans. It's refreshing. Each time I see a wild animal, I feel like I've experienced direct contact with God or the universal force that made all this.

After several minutes of rolling around in the pleasure of getting to see the elusive bobcat and her kit, I continued to ease Pearl up the road and took the fork right.

I just kept feeling that I needed to go right. I didn't care where I went. After getting to stare into the eyes of a bobcat and watch her kit play, I would've slept in a parking lot.

I arrived at a right turn that looked like it would take me to an overlook. We bounced down the pockmarked road, and then one last left and there it was. There was the reason I'd been led here, after all. I couldn't believe it. How was it even possible? Of the thousands of miles of land and forest, how could I've landed here?

I felt like a little kid, not wanting to wait for the car to stop before I got out. I slid to a stop and the sound made her turn towards me.

I felt like I'd looked into those eyes thousands of times. Her teeth shimmered in the light. I opened the van door, turned off the lights, and scooted out of the seat.

"Hi! What are you doing here?"

Sara

I looked up from my dock bed and felt compelled to turn my head east. Suddenly a mammoth ball of fire exploded in the sky, followed by three smaller ones. My lungs collapsed.

"Joel?" I murmured.

"Yes, I saw it too." He whispered back.

Joel had insisted on accompanying me back to the farm and staying as long as his body would allow. In the dark moonless night, his arms wrapped around my shoulders and his hands held mine. My lungs could only take in wisps of air. They, like me, didn't want to accept the fate we'd been dealt. It felt so unfair that I couldn't stay in Ilanaly, and not a cell of my body wanted to accept it.

"What was that?" I'd returned to my habit of talking out loud. Joel responded in kind.

"It was a meteor coming through the atmosphere. I've never seen one. Only heard about them."

"I've never seen one so big. It looked like two jetliners crashed."

The sky was so dark that the stars almost touched. Now and then a star would dance across the sky, like they were showing off. But this explosion felt more like an omen.

Joel squeezed me and kissed my head. "I've got to go back." He whispered in my ear.

The tears started flowing down my face. Like the earth's springs, I wasn't sure they'd ever stop.

I turned to face him, not knowing if I'd ever get to kiss his lips or hold his face in my hands again. "Wherever you are Sara, I'm here." He pointed to my heart. "I can hear you, you're never alone."

"Really? You'll be able to hear me from here?"

He laughed. "Yes." He gave me one last kiss, and slipped into the blackened waters, like leaving quickly was going to make it easier for me. He was gone. My head tugged toward the waters, hoping for one last glance.

I stared at the spot, holding myself back from jumping in. I hugged my arms across my chest and knees, sobbing relentlessly. And just like so many times before, when despair took over, I felt a wet, warm tongue slide up my cheek.

There sat that big goofy face looking into my eyes with his "I'm here too" grin.

Clem had found me at the dock. Mom had been caring for him, but he seemed to know I'd come back. I wrapped my arms around his neck. His hugs were the furry equivalent of Joel. His licks tumbled me backward and I fell asleep, like so many times with his head resting next to mine.

***

I woke up as the first light hit my eye lids. But it wasn't the same. I felt like a flash of light in this enormous universe. No body to drag around. I was an ant in the universal rainforest. I had no edges. And the Universe was infinite. I knew all this from my studies, but I could FEEL it. There was no gravity. My feet touched the ground, but they melted with the air particles. I was a speck of light, among trillions of floating specks. I could feel the enormity of the world in a way I'd never experienced. Not just Earth. All of it. The galaxies, the lifetimes, the infiniteness of space. I felt so much release. The earth was giving me a welcome home gift. Clem looked the same but there was no division between our cells. It was like our minds made up the boundaries. They didn't REALLY exist.

The air was thick with wet warmth. The Goldfinches were bouncing off the purple thistles and the Towhees were scraping the ground for grubs. I loved Ilanaly, but I missed the solidity of life on earth, the smell of decaying wood and the bird songs that had been my daily alarm clock.

I danced through the woods, Clem at my side, saying hello to all my friends.

Did Mema know about Ilanaly? Was that why the pond was built there? Is that why she and Mom had made sure this property was protected? Maybe it wasn't just about the trees after all?

Mema was from a prominent Boston family, but when she married my grandad, she left all the fancy parties and afternoon teas behind. It'd never really suited her. Granddad lived in the woods, and they just met by chance one day when they were at the same store buying supplies. Mema smiled at Granddad. They married soon after that.

My grandparents came across the states in a buggy Mema's dad gave them as a wedding present. I don't think he thought they'd take it to the other side of the country. My mema wasn't afraid of anything. If she was, she never showed it. She could talk the bow and arrow off an Indian's back. She made friends wherever she went. The natives taught her how to make clothes from hides, how to use every part of the animal they killed and to bless them and give thanks.

Halfway across the US, she became pregnant with my uncle. They decided they needed to find a nice place to settle down.

When I was 16, many years after Mema died, I asked Mom how they'd found this place.

"I'm not sure." She shrugged. "There were stories of her being guided here."

***

After a few hours the ecstasy wore off. I hoped I'd stay that way. But when I started thinking about heading to the house my fearful thoughts took over where once was space.

Clem and I wandered toward the house, slowing to a tip toe as we got close. I hid behind the trees so I could see whose cars were in the driveway. I let out a deep sigh when I saw it was just Mom's. I stayed tucked in the trees as I walked around the back. Mom was putting the week's laundry on the clothesline.

Clem kept by my side, while I took a few deep breaths and thought about what to tell Mom. She was going to wonder where I'd been. Luckily, she was used to me being gone weeks at a time. This time was different, I wasn't at a job. *Did I tell her about Ilanaly and Brian? Surely, he'd told her by now.*

Ilanaly was like a child's hiding spot where I hid all my treasures that I didn't want my parents or brother to find and tell me I had to get rid of them. And yet Mom was the first person I'd told about the trees talking to me, and she was fascinated, in fact she didn't even seem surprised. I should've guessed then that she had her own secrets.

I took one last deep breath and walked toward Mom. I stood tall and determined. I wasn't going to let her or anyone else get to Ilanaly. I was even more determined to keep Brian and his money making schemes off this property whether or not I had Mom's support.

I just wished I'd known how she was going to respond when I told her.

Clem got to her first and rubbed his head on her thigh.

"Well, there you are." Mom put down the basket of wet clothes and rubbed his ears. "Let's get you some breakfast." She started for the house.

"Hey Mom." I waved.

She stopped in mid-stride and pivoted toward me. Clem sat next to her as if to say 'I was trying to tell ya".

"Sara!"

She walked over to me and wrapped her arms around my neck, like I'd just returned from war. "I'm so glad you're back." Tears trickled down her cheeks. "I thought maybe Clem went out to find you. Let me get you both some breakfast."

Her eyes glowed. I'd never seen her so happy to see me before. What was going on?

"Mom, can we talk first? I want to tell you where I've been."

"Sure, sure, let me get Clem some food and we can sit on the porch."

While Mom tended to Clem I sat on the swing. My cheeks seemed to be permanently attached to smiling. I'd lived here for over 30 years and yet everything looked brighter. It was like it'd gotten a fresh coat of paint while I was gone. It was almost noon, and the sun was just starting to heat up the water filled air. The morning clouds had lost again as they often do in July around here. The dozens of hummingbirds that called this home in the warm months, were fighting over the feeders again. Every year we'd put out a dozen feeders all around the yard, so they all had a chance to feed. Grandad had created an ingenious pulley system, so all the bird feeders were well out of the bear's reach.

Mom sat next to me on the swing Grandad made for Mema to fit this screened porch. "This is a beautiful skirt, Sara!" Mom rubbed the folds of the skirt as they wrapped around my crossed legs.

I put my hand on hers and looked into her eyes and took a deep breath. "Mom, I don't know how to explain where I've been. I'm afraid to tell you, and yet I want you to know."

She put her hand on top of mine and smiled at me. "Did you find the rock in the pond?"

I bolted up and stood over her. "You know?" My happiness was plunging into anger.

She just continued smiling at me. "Oh Sara, you can't imagine what a relief it is that you found it. That the rock presented itself to you."

"But why didn't you tell me? You know what a difference it would have made had I known sooner, if I'd had people around who didn't think I was crazy? Even YOU would tell me to stop talking about the trees and play with dolls like the other kids."

She patted the seat next to her. "I'm sorry. I couldn't tell you. It has to find you. I'm surprised you didn't see it sooner."

The last time I'd seen Mom filled with such remorse is when Mema died.

I paced back and forth across the porch. Clem came in to see what the ruckus was about. He looked at me with those loving eyes he had when he knew I felt alone. "Then why didn't you at least help me feel I was normal for spending so much time in the woods? Why didn't you defend me?"

She took a deep breath and looked out to the trees. "I was jealous." She responded, barely audible.

I collapsed in the seat next to her, all the anger pushed out. "Jealous of what?"

She hung her head down. "I wanted to live like you. And at the same time, I wanted you to fit in. I know that loneliness and I didn't want you to experience it too."

I fell to the floor. Everything I thought I knew was wrong.

Clem and Mom both joined me on the floor. "I'm sorry." Mom said as she looked at my eyes.

The smile returned to my face.

Maxine

"Hi!"

"What are you doing way out here?" I looked at Molly in shock, hoping my voice didn't betray my excitement.

"Well, I could ask you the same thing. I didn't know anyone knew about this place." Her long brown hair was pulled into a haphazard ponytail.

I shrugged my shoulders. "I didn't know about it-just seemed to be led here, I guess."

Molly nodded with a smile and waved her hand toward the view. The stars were so thick you could fall right into them. We sat on a ponderosa pine log that had been enjoying this view for decades.

No wonder he didn't decay. Who'd want to leave this place?

Molly broke the moments of silence. "So really you got all the way up here, just by using your intuition? How does that work?" Her worn t-shirt and cut-off shorts smelled like smoke. That burned wood smell trickled out of her pores.

"I really don't know." I shrugged my shoulders. "It's like a sound and an internal nudge all at the same time." But I have to be quiet, or I'll miss it. There's no force to it, it's like a suggestion of something you can choose or not." I went back to staring at the stars. "Really, I'm just figuring this out myself. A friend suggested that's how I'd find Sara." I wanted to kick myself for bringing up Sara again. *Why did her name keep popping out of my mouth?*

Molly's smiling face disappeared. I was afraid she'd take off again. *Please, please,* I said to myself, *don't let her leave.*

"Sorry I brought that up again. There seems to be something about that name that bothers you," I responded quietly.

Weird, right, talking to a stranger this way? But Molly didn't feel like a stranger. She felt like someone I'd known for more than just this life, like I'd known her for lifetimes, like I'd never NOT known her. *You ever meet someone like that?*

She sat motionless, staring at her worn Keene sandals.

"So you're not working tonight?" Changing the subject seemed the best thing to do.

"No, it's my night off. I feel silly. The fire rages on and we have to take time off. The animals and trees aren't getting a break. Why should I?" Molly looked off in what I assumed was the direction of the fire. "But them's the rules. I'm so used to being out there at night I couldn't sleep at camp, so I walked up here."

"That's quite a hike."

"Well, I wasn't carrying any gear. I ran most of it. I'm used to it." Like hiking 10 miles in the dark without a trail was the most normal thing in the world.

"Ran! That hill is almost straight up!"

"I've done worse carrying 30 pounds of gear." She was so nonchalant about her abilities.

I looked back at Molly, so glad she was still there and trying hard not to say anything that would make her leave again. "I'm curious. Why do you fight wildfires? Wouldn't it be safer to work in a town, or even jump out of planes for a living? You guys die, and it's gotta be a painful death." I couldn't help but ask.

"I know. I'm just obsessed with this work, ever since I saw my first wildland jumper. The smokiness of his clothes, the dirt across his face, the wildness of his hair. His eyes were fierce but calm and sure. There wasn't anything he couldn't do. He'd seen the worst and fought it back. I wanted that. I'd been living in the woods most of my life. Why not protect them if I could?" She smiled, seeming to transport herself back to that time.

I didn't want to change the subject, but I really wanted to know why she'd lived in the woods.

"Wait, what? You lived in the woods most of your life?"

"Oh, yeah, guess I let that slip out. I don't tell most people that." She sat up suddenly, her shoulders twisted, and her eyes looked straight into mine. "Who are you? Have we met before?"

I shrugged. "I know, it feels like we're twins separated at birth or something. Right? I've always wanted a sister, and you feel like her."

"Yes!! Exactly! You feel like the sister I knew I had, but no one could tell me where you were!"

We laughed and hugged while the stars hugged us.

Sara

"Morning, Sara. Sorry to call you away from your chores. Sorry to hear about your job and all." The county sheriff had shown up on our doorstep the day after my return.

Mom, always the hostess, had invited Sheriff Brinson in and given him some coffee, even though he couldn't be here to help us.

"What can we do for you?" I asked reluctantly. The man was once a friend, but I could tell he wasn't there to see how I was. I felt like an intruder was sitting at our kitchen table.

"Well, your mom seemed to think you ought to hear this straight from me." He smiled at her.

"Sara, wait till you hear this!" Mom grabbed my arm, making me bump into one of the kitchen chairs, as she fought back tears. It was taking an iron-will for her to stay upright in her seat.

"What's this about?" I glared at her, annoyed with her playing the victim.

"Well, your brother Brian is claiming you and I are trying to steal his land." She said it like I needed to know which brother was causing problems.

"What are you talking about?"

I confronted the sheriff. "Mom owns this land and when she's gone, she's deeded it to me. Brian's always wanting to take what's his-and take what's not his."

"Well, you know...." He replied, looking back and forth between Mom and me, "land usually goes to the first-born son around here, not the daughters. Usually, they go and live on their husband's land."

I knew he was trying to devalue me for not being a 'normal' girl, but I cared more about protecting this farm than about what he thought of me.

"FUCK!!" I leaned over and slammed a hand on the table.

"Sara!" Mom yelled back. "Watch your mouth, you're not around those logger boys. Show him respect." Mom had no problem reprimanding me.

I paced back and forth across the kitchen, "Sheriff, this is bullshit and you know it. Mom, can give the land to whomever she wants, and she wants me to have it-just like her mom wanted her to have it!" I was trying hard to not throw something.

"Well, Brian thinks you've coerced her somehow. That you're forcing her to keep him off, on account of all that tree stuff." The Sheriff couldn't look me in the eye. It was if he thought I'd turn him into a toad. *And a part of me wished I could.*

"And just how would I do that?" I replied, not batting an eye.

"I don know. But Brian has a point. It's just not normal for the land to go to the girls."

"Not normal for here, maybe!"

"Sara, watch your manners. I apologize, Sheriff."

"That's okay. Endured worse. So ma'am is Sara forcing you?" The Sheriff looked at her like he was trying to tell her it was okay to admit I was forcing her to give me the land.

"Of course not. I'm giving it to Sara because I promised my mother I'd protect her trees and only Sara will do that." Mom put her rattling coffee cup down.

The Sheriff took the last bite of the peach bread Mom had served him.

He looked out the screened porch. "I'm gonna need to take a look around a bit, if you don't mind." Like he was really asking our permission.

I glared into his eyes. "I do mind, Sheriff. We haven't done anything wrong."

Mom patted my hand and looked at me, trying to hold back her tears.

"Well then, there's no reason I can't take a look then. Brian seems to think you're hiding something in the pond you don't want him to have."

I filled my lungs with air and forced my wobbling legs to stay upright. "Sorry Sheriff, we're not hiding anything. If you want to look around, you'll need a warrant."

Mom's glossy eyes stayed focused on me as she squeezed my hand, trying to find her courage.

The bird's songs and cricket chirps filled the silent air.

The Sheriff peered at me and nodded his head. "This don't help your case none."

I held his gaze. "There isn't a case."

"Well, now, I'm sorry, but I'm gonna have to talk with the county attorney about this. I just need to see if this is legal and all."

"How can it not be legal? It's my property and I can give it to who I want. AND it's MY property right now. I'm sole owner."

"I hear you, but I just don't know if you have the legal standing to keep Brian off the land."

"There's no LAW that says Mom has to give her property to her first-born son or even let him on it. It's just tradition around here." I was having a hard time staying in the room with all this ignorance.

"Well, I'm gonna have to check on a few things. For now, you have no legal standing to keep Brian off this property." He took a last sip of coffee and stood up, ignoring my words.

"THAT'S CRAZY!!" I yelled. Mom owns this property. Doesn't even have a mortgage! *She* can say who she can and cannot have on the property."

"Well maybe, maybe not. I'll get back to you as soon as I can see things clear." His grin betrayed him.

"That'll be never," I grumbled to Mom.

"Sara! Watch your mouth. I will not have you talking to the authorities like that. He's just doing his job. And we'll do ours." She winked at me.

The sheriff tipped his hat to Mom, then me, put his hand on his side arm and soldiered back to his car.

I held my breath until I couldn't see his car any longer.

I yelled into the air, calling up every curse word I knew.

"Sara!!! You've got to stop that cursing." Mom began picking up the dishes and cups from the Sheriff's visit, putting them in the sink.

"Mom! How can you not swear? You've got these people telling you who you can and cannot let on your property."

"It doesn't matter, we both know there's no law saying Brian can be here when he wants. You know he'll try everything he can. This was his home."

"I know, but now he wants to destroy it. Who destroys something they consider their home?" I got to work on the dirty dishes. It was good to have something to do with my hands even though it was hard on the china.

"Well, you've got a point there," Mom said slowly, her head drooping. "Do you have any ideas?" She sounded like she was exhausted and just wanted to curl into a hole.

"Yes." The clank of clean dishes going into the drying rack punctuated my words. "We can hire a lawyer to show there's no law that tells you who you can give your land to. I'm not letting him destroy Ilanaly. He'll have to destroy me first." I put a soapy hand to my forehead.

"Well, you know he might just try to do that," Mom whispered.

"I wish Joel was here," I mumbled, thinking about his calmness.

Mom's head perked up. "Who's Joel?"

"Oh, in all the craziness, I totally forgot to tell you!" I put the last dish into the sink.

Suddenly tears started rolling down my face. I wondered if I'd ever get to see him again.

Sara

I sat under the Wonder tree, as I had so many times when I needed to feel whole and loved and seen. Even before I was hearing her talk, I felt her branches were the most loving arms. No judgment, no telling me what I should or shouldn't do. Just silent understanding. Those are the best friendships, aren't they? The ones that don't require words?

After the Sheriff's visit yesterday, Mom and I sat on the screened porch, and I told her all about Joel. My heart fluttered and my bones stiffened when I talked about him. It was like my body was holding me back from where my heart wanted to go.

"Right now, I'd really love it if you'd tell me what to do,' I said to the 40 foot round Douglas fir that I'd dubbed Wonder Tree when I was only five years old. It seemed like the most normal name for her. When I told my family about it, Brian immediately started calling her Chainsawed, just to torment me.

Quiet. She knew there were no words that would help me right now. This was a decision I had to make, and only I could decide, though I desperately wanted help. My lungs slowly took in the gentle breezes that fluttered around her outstretched arms.

After perfect moments, she contributed to the calm. "Whatever you decide, Sara, will be okay. There's nothing wrong here. It may seem like it for a short time, but whatever decision you make will only be a blip in time. A minute. Like a pinhead amongst the stars."

It didn't really help to know my decision would have so little meaning over time. In fact, it felt worse. I felt stupid for making such a big deal out of it. It felt huge to me. But I also got what she was really saying was that it was okay. Yes, it would have an effect now, but I didn't need to put so much pressure on myself. There were a lot of bigger forces at work here.

I remembered waking up one morning, and feeling my body was nothing more than a flash of light amid twinkling space. I felt so small and yet important at the same time. I felt like I was in a playbox, and nothing I did and everything I did was important at the same time. That each action would reverberate into the whole but at the same time that reverberation was so insignificant in the scheme of it all. I'd never felt so much joy and bubbly lightness than I did during that time. I weighed an ounce and laughter surrounded me. A playground of fun. I remembered who I truly was, unburdened by my worries and fears, untethered by thoughts. Love, so much love. Okayness surrounded by light. And as light constantly moves and changes so does this life. I could feel how big the Universe was. Not just Earth. All of it. The galaxies, the lifetimes, the infiniteness of time. It was like being a water droplet in the midst of the ocean. I had no edges, no beginning or end. I was a beam of light amongst a soup of love. I danced around for hours in delight. But the burdens slowly squelched the light. It was a taste of Ilanaly before I even knew it existed.

When I'm feeling overwhelmed by life, I remember that moment, those hours, and how little effect what I did had. I wasn't in charge. God was. I just felt love. All there was was love and joy. It was reassuring in those days, when it felt like I had really messed up. That I hadn't lived my life the way I was supposed to. And it was freeing to feel so insignificant, that someone else, much wiser than I, was at the helm. This was what Wonder Tree was telling me now. Yes, in the short term, there would be repercussions to my decision, but, in the grand scheme of things, everything was going to work out. Because none of this was real. Only love was.

"Wonder Tree?"

Silence. She used her words wisely.

"How do I let people know how important trees are to us? How important it is to have elder trees like you around? That you're the ones that teach the young how to thrive when times get tough? How do I help people to be quiet and hear your wisdom, and feel that you were put here to help us? Not only to turn our exhales into inhales, but show us how community truly works. Helping everyone, no matter how different they may be from us?"

"By your life, Sara. You can't tell people what to think and do. They have to experience it and decide for themselves." Her voice was a singing melody.

I didn't like her answer, but I knew she was right.

That's what I really wanted people to know and experience. If they'd just stop and listen to the trees, if they'd just be still and quiet when they were outside. If they could just realize how important the trees are to us having clean air. The wisdom they carry inside themselves of how to fight against diseases, passing that knowledge on to their offspring. How they help everyone, not just themselves. Their roots benefit other plants. Their branches support numerous wildlife. They truly represent community-even a single tree provides so much. They put back so much more than they take.

I wish Wonder Tree's words had helped more than they did. I wish I didn't feel the tension in my belly. I wish I could've gotten my shoulders to relax for more than a minute. I remembered that none of my really good decisions had been made with my mind. I made them in a flash of inspiration, when I was pushed past thinking, because the words didn't help.

I molded my back to Wonder Tree's red felt bark, letting the streams murmur soothe my fiery nerves. The steady sound reminded me of the answers that come, even when I can't see them from here.

Maxine

The next morning, she was gone. Like a wild animal, hiding before the dawn.

My neck was stiff, and I was wet from dew. We'd talked about nothing until we fell asleep against the hard log.

I never found out where she was from, how she'd lived outside or with who. My questions of her led to more questions about myself. Like she knew I'd take the hook.

I shook off the last of my sleep and got out my little MSR stove to make some instant coffee. I wanted to find Molly not dally with food.

After my cup was full of black wakefulness, I gathered my stuff and slid into Pearl's driver's seat. *Okay, intuition*, I thought to myself, *don't leave me now. Where is Molly?*

I followed what I thought were nudges down the road toward the fire camp. I looked at the city of tents. It was a ghost-town. No sign of Molly-or anyone else.

I parked on the far edges of the woods, away from the camp, and walked around, hoping to find someone. But someone had come in and taken all the bodies, all the life, and left only tents.

In the distance was a huge white circus-like tent, looking like it had accidentally landed here. *Oh, they must be eating breakfast!* I thought to myself.

I wandered over, feeling silly and excited. A schoolgirl's crush. The dried ground crunching under my Teva's was the only sound. No voices from the tent, no clacking of dishes. I shook. Not even the birds were chirping today.

An exhaustless truck zoomed down the main road as I inched myself toward the giant white canopy. Silence.

I walked through the wide opening of the three-sided tent. There sat rows and rows of plastic tables and metal chairs. All waiting for someone to come. I bit my lip, feeling like I'd been left at the pound, no longer wanted.

Then I heard a familiar noise. The faint sound of running water. I followed the sound to the back of the tent.

A plump man with a dirty white apron over his t-shirt and jeans bent over a makeshift plastic sink.

"Do you know Molly?" I blurted.

The man straightened up rapidly and looked at me. "Yeah, of course." Like he wasn't even surprised I was there.

"Have you seen her this morning?" I asked abruptly, totally forgetting my manners

"No, haven't seen her for a couple days. Not unusual though, those kids work some weird shifts." He returned to washing the dishes and ignoring me.

I hurried back to the tent town and walked around more. "Molly", I gently called, afraid I'd wake up someone besides her.

"Molly... it's Max...you here?" whispering as loudly as I could.

Where was everyone? I heard a door slam in the porta potty area, so I ran to the sound.

Walking toward me was an ash-covered man, body slumped, like he could barely stand up.

"Hey, you know Molly?" I blurted.

His eyes narrowed as he looked my way.

"Why are you asking about Molly?" He continued to stare and walk toward me. I wished I hadn't asked.

I stumbled in response. "Well, we were camping out last night and she left before I could say bye."

He gave me a sideways glance. His eyes laid into mine, searching for something. "What are you doing here anyway? You don't look like you're crew." He walked closer, and I inched back.

"No, sorry, I'm not..." I stammered, "just found this place and then met Molly." I kept feeling for the earth behind me with my toes.

"Well, this area for crew only. You need to leave." His right index finger pointed toward the road.

"I just want to find Molly."

"I think it's time you leave," he growled and took a big step toward me.

My lungs closed and the earth trembled. I stumbled around and willed my noodly legs toward Pearl.

What is with all this secrecy stuff around here? They really don't like you asking about others, I thought as I made my way up the road and to my car.

Monster Man was watching my every step. I could feel his eyes piercing my skull.

Having forgotten to breathe the last few minutes, I gulped in air the moment I reached for Pearl's door handle. I slid in the driver's seat and dropped my forehead on the steering wheel. Tears poured out my heart. I felt like I'd just misplaced my best friend, even though I'd only known her a day. "Where are you, Molly?" I whispered to the air. "Please help me find Molly," I said as I looked up to the cloudless sky.

Sara

The shimmering rock in the pond was pulling me as I floated over her. I'd swam past that hole to heaven everyday since my conversation with Wonder Tree two weeks ago. Allowing her words to soothe my ache. I longed for a dramaless day with Joel.

Brian had gotten fired from his job because he was telling people about what he saw in Ilanaly and about the interactions he saw me have with the trees and animals. The company decided Brian had lost it, and it was time to let him go.

He blamed me.

"If you'd let me show people, then they'd see I wasn't crazy! But NOOOO, you gotta' keep it all to yourself. Dear precious Sara can't hurt anything," he mocked.

Brian had been trying for weeks to get back into Ilanaly. He even showed up with a bulldozer in the middle of the night to try to undo the repairs we'd made to the pond. Since then we'd gotten a court order to keep him off the property. It wasn't what we wanted, but he was so fixated on getting back into Ilanaly.

I'd given up hoping he'd ever change. I so wanted us to be close. To love and support each other. But he chose resentment instead.

The day he got fired, he left a message on Mom's answering machine, yelling at the top of his lungs. "You and that Sara have ruined my life. It's YOUR fault they fired me. You just wait, I'm gonna show 'em!"

I used to resent his jealousy-until I discovered Ilanaly. Something about that place just made everything feel fine. Like the little spats and the jealousy were so insignificant, not even real. They were just things we made up in our minds. These were the things I wanted people to know. These were the things I'd tried to share with others.

These were all the thoughts floating through my head when I first saw the smoke.

My heart jumped and so did my legs.

I ran to my truck as quickly as I could, having no idea what I could do, but I couldn't just stand there and watch the smoke. It looked like it was on Hutton's land. How was that possible?

Bessie grumbled to a start and bumped down our dirt road. I looked around to see if I had so much as a water can in the truck. I didn't. I kept going.

After a very long 20 minutes, I came to the road and gate. I knew how to get onto the Hutton's land, but I wasn't supposed to since I was no longer working. I stared for a moment at the combo lock on the gate, bit my lip, and began to input the combination I'd entered hundreds of times, but the lock fell in my hand. My heart skipped. We never left these locks open.

I looked around for a second, half thinking a mob of people were gonna jump on me, but nothing. No one was there, not so much as a siren.

I swung open the gates and left them that way, thinking the fire trucks would be coming behind.

Bessie used every bit of her ability to get up the sharply curved roads just wide enough for the logging trucks. This area hadn't been logged in many years, the snowy winters and rainy falls had made it barely drivable.

When I got within eyeshot of the fire, I grabbed my thick canvas Carhartt coat and gloves, put on my sunglasses to shield my eyes, and ran empty-handed toward the fire. It must have been there, the truck, but I didn't see it. I just wanted to get the fire out. That these trees were on the chopping block didn't occur to me. I couldn't let the animals die this way. Death by fire must be the most horrible way to die.

As I reached the fire's edge, I noticed a pack of matches and empty gas can on the ground.

"Why would anyone do this?" I yelled to the sky, my heart racing, my arms thrusting upwards, and my bones feeling like noodles. I knew these woods. I'd walked them dozens of times. The Hutton's did selective logging, not clear-cut. I found Clem not far from here, when I was marking trees about 7 years ago.

I ran to a stream about 100 yards away, one of the never-ending waterways that spring from the earth.

Now I'm about to tell you what happened. You're probably not going to believe me. I wouldn't believe me if I hadn't been there. I hadn't expected it. I didn't know this was possible here. But somehow it was. It must've been Joel helping me.

I kneeled. "Water, please help me!!" I don't know why I asked. I just didn't know what else to do. I just needed that water on the fire somehow.

And that's when it started. There was no fanfare, no rumble, no sign of what was to come. The gravity of the earth shifted under the water. The artist suddenly decided to paint the water going up instead of going down. The untethered liquid danced like a fire hose that disconnected from its hydrant. I pointed to the flames. 'That way, please put out the fire,' I pleaded. I fell back as the stream rose and flowed above my head, as if it did this kind of thing all the time. I was giddy. It was just what I'd seen in Ilanaly.

The skyborne faucet soared up to the treetops and poured down on the killing flames. Droplets from the stream caressed my cheeks along with my tears. Hissing from the doused flames rolled from under natures' faucet. The play unfolded, nature taking care of itself. *How is this possible?* The once gurgling creek was now a firehose in the hands of the most adept firefighter. It gushed all over the half acre fire. Wherever my eyes went, the streamhose would follow. It was freaky. Even though I'd seen this happen in Ilanaly, it happening here, in this 3D world, was bizarre. As soon as the last ember was dark, the water shrank back into the earth and acted like nothing had happened.

"Thank you," I whispered to the waters. "Thank you," I quavered in awe and disbelief.

"You're welcome," they whispered back.

I collapsed, lying in stunned silence, trying to comprehend what I'd just seen, feeling my breath fill up my lungs once again-my heart return to its normal beat.

Thump, thump...thump, thump...

I'd seen the waters in Ilanaly rolling about willy-nilly, but how did that happen here? *Here on earth?* How did my request for help turn the creek into a fire hose?

"It was you, Sara. Thank you for saving us," the trees sang.

Suddenly there was a crashing of branches and the roar of a truck screeching down the road I'd come up. The sound of the truck was familiar. One I'd heard hundreds of times throughout my life, but it couldn't be. It just wasn't possible.

Please, please, please don't let it be possible.

Maxine

The sun was glowing orange and red as it started lighting up the other side of the planet. Not a good sign. The smoke from the fire was getting worse, not better. *Maybe Molly had gone back out to help.*

I had stayed parked in the same spot all day that day, hoping Molly would come by. I hadn't realized how isolated I felt until I met Molly. She was the first friend I'd made on this trip that was my age. I'd gotten so used to being around people who knew me growing up, I didn't realize how lonely I'd get with so much unaccompanied time. It did help me to know myself a little better. I'd never realized how lucky I was to grow up around such kind people. Just realizing that, was a good enough reason to come on this trip. It helped me to appreciate what I had. The conversations with Molly allowed me to see myself better through her eyes. I said things that I didn't even know were true, things I didn't know I believed. Things about knowing in my heart that nature was here to help us, and we as humans had to take good care of her. I shared with her about how comfortable I felt in the woods, and how deeply connected I felt to the stars. It turned out, she felt the same way. I'd never talked to anyone about this, I was afraid of what they'd think, but I didn't feel that way with Molly. She was like the earth itself, confident and sure. It was freeing to meet someone who felt about things the way I did. I was looking forward to getting to know her better. She was a beacon of the independence I was struggling to find. And on top of that, there was an inkling that maybe she knew Sara. It seemed almost impossible that I'd randomly meet someone else who knew the author of the notebook, but this trip had been one miracle after another when I listened to my inner voice.

That was four days ago and no sign of Molly. Someone who I'd only known for a day left a vast hole in my life when she disappeared. Why did she just leave? Why all the secrecy about Sara and Molly's whereabouts?

I kept an eye on tent town during the days, hoping for a glimpse of Molly, but she didn't appear. I felt my intuition had failed me. I so wanted to live from my heart instead of my mind, but this time it had brought me intense pain.

It would've been fine if Monster Man just said he couldn't tell me where Molly was, but he looked like he wanted to cut out my tongue. What was I missing? A part of me felt like I needed to move on, but I didn't want to leave. I'd gotten to know this place, and I felt a strange connection to the crew even though Molly and Monster Man were the only ones I talked to. I didn't dare go back. It was clear I wasn't welcome.

It was scary to leave a place I'd gotten to know. I felt safe there. People have this strange idea that I'm brave because I'm wandering all around the countryside by myself. I don't feel brave, I just feel I'm following some invisible path. Some days, I just wish I knew where it was going. Most of the time, I love just traveling and seeing where I end up for the night. But then there are times when the desire to know where I'll be sleeping will wash through me. I can't really afford campgrounds, plus they're noisy. When I feel like that, what I really want is to be able to afford a Four Seasons Hotel suite. But then the stars come out, the quiet overtakes the heat, and I just feel like the luckiest person on earth.

One more night, I promised myself. *She may show up tonight.*

Sara

A week had passed since the fire on the Hutton's land. I'd not seen or heard from Brian. I spent my days and nights walking around our farm, checking for Brian's presence and keeping an eye on the pond.

Every time I saw that glistening rock covering the most beautiful place I'd seen, I'd have to hold myself back from just jumping into the waters and back to Joel's arms.

I was starting to relax, thinking maybe that fire on Hutton's place was just a fluke. That some traveler had accidentally started it. *California had people terrorizing the logging lands, but we seemed to be immune to it up here. Maybe they'd spread out.*

***

On Wednesday, exactly eight days after the last fire, I woke up to one of the scariest smells a woodland person ever experiences. Smoke. This wasn't campfire smoke, this was billowing smoke. It sent terror through my veins. Smoke on a dry summer's day can mean the end of the homes for hundreds of animals and humans in an instant.

As I ran toward the smoke, an image flashed through my mind of the burned area near Mount St. Helen's Volcanic eruption. The devastation. It looked like hundreds of bombs had gone off. I was asked to go in and find the salvageable trees so they could be hauled out. When I walked through trying to find something that wasn't just char, I thought of all the bunnies that used to play here. All the chipmunks, snakes, and golden mantle ground squirrels who were likely seared to death. My aunt's home, with photos from 100 years ago, and irreplaceable paintings from my mema became a black pile of rubble.

It was an eerie feeling being amongst all that dead. I imagined Hiroshima and what those people endured. Not as many human lives were lost in the wildfire, but it didn't make it any less painful.

During that time on Mount St. Helens, I felt like I was on sacred ground. Ground where a great massacre occurred. There's a hollow feeling and sound. No matter if cars are going by or planes overhead, there's just this somber quiet. A funeral where people are afraid to say anything. A graveyard where the corpses are standing upright. I tiptoed across the scorched ground whispering, "I'm sorry, I'm sorry" with every step. I'd heard accounts of the excruciating pain of burn victims, and I feared I was causing a similar pain to the mute earth.

Sometimes, when I see an overwhelming amount of pain, I have to turn away. So I stayed away from burned areas. I thought there was nothing to be done. It's like being on the front lines of a battlefield or going to a hospital filled with sick people. It's overwhelming, even for the medical team. Where do we put the sorrow and helpless feeling?

Even back then, I felt like I was being shown something. Like I was supposed to do something more than just mark the trees. I had no inkling that I'd be led to what I'm doing now. It turned out I was being taken down a path, a journey of action and helping and making a difference. Over the next few years, I started slowly seeing that my inaction, my fear of what others would think, was almost as bad as the actions of those who didn't understand the importance of the trees and nature.

***

Feeling Clem's slobber tickle my ankle, suddenly brought me back to the black pillows of rising smoke.

Worse than smelling smoke, was seeing exactly where it was coming from. Eagle Tree. Bald Eagles had been nesting there for decades. There were babies in that nest now.

As I ran up the hill, I kept telling myself *there's no way he could set her on fire!* It would take more than a few matches to light up the majestic Incense Cedar. She was over 200 feet tall and 8 feet in diameter. Her hard-ridged, sweet cinnamon bark was made to withstand fires.

I was wrong.

All the bushes and saplings at her feet were ablaze. Her bark was putting up a battle, but could only hold the flames off for a few minutes. My belly constricted and my eyes widened. *How in the hell could he do this? These trees did nothing to him!*

"Eagle Tree!" I screamed. "Help me! I want to save your babies. I don't know how!" I yelled as I threw handfuls of dirt on the flames as quickly as I could. Clem followed suit using his front paws.

"Sara, you know exactly what to do." She responded in the tone of a Buddhist monk. Shortly after I started hearing the trees, I asked them how they felt about being cut and dying in fires. Their answer shocked me. "We are eternal, just like you. This is only one life, one time, one choice. We're not really dead. It just looks it to you. The loss is yours, your humanity, not ours."

The searing heat quickly brought me back. "This is no time for riddles, please just tell me what to do!" Tears cooled my burning skin.

"The creek, Sara, ask the creek for help."

"What? The creek is half a mile away! I can't get there and back in time." I fell to my knees, overwhelm shut off my brain.

"Sara, listen. Listen with your heart. You know what to do." Her voice was a balm among the explosion in my ears of the pop and crackling of the plants at her feet.

I tried to tune out the killing sounds. I tried to find that quiet place.

"I can't. It's too noisy here. I can't think with all the noise." I put my fists against my ears.

"You can." There was no anger or frustration in her voice. It was almost as if she didn't care if I put the fire out or not. It wasn't her job. Her job was to stand calmly in the middle of the chaos and send love, so much love.

I fell to the ground in a heap. Clem kept digging up dirt.

As I laid on the ground, with my eyes closed to the inferno, I felt a Q tip touch the tip of my nose. It was soft and pointed. Not demanding, but certain. I wasn't sure I was feeling anything, but a pine needle prick. Then I heard the familiar sound. A sound that had brought me dancing joy for decades. The sound I loved so much that I carried a feeder full of sugar water with me on all my treks.

A buzz. Not the buzz of a bee, but the purring buzz of a hummingbird! I cocked my head and opened my eyes and there looking through my eyes and into my heart was the glistening red and purple of a magnificent hummingbird. She poured all the strength and courage she used to fly thousands of miles each year into me and filled every cell of my body. "You can do it, Sara," came a high-pitched whisper. I exploded with joy. Every cell tingled, and glowed. The boundaries in my mind shattered and was filled with light and space. I felt watched over and loved. First flying waters and now a hummingbird poke.

The hummingbird and I remained beak to nose. Seconds passed as I let her encouragement pour over me. Then I remembered. I had done it in Ilanaly. Joel had taught me. *Was it really possible to do that here?*

"Yes." I heard his voice. "It's in you."

I felt like I was underwater in the pond. Where all the distractions above can't touch me and are muted. I was in a bubble of silent stillness. I could use my mind. I didn't have to go to the creek.

I slowly looked up into my head, with my eyes closed, took a deep breath and imagined the water from the creek rushing over and putting out the flames. I felt the wetness falling from above, squelching the flames. I felt how grateful I would be when all was quiet and green again.

"That's it, Sara," said the jeweled bird.

I remained in my bubble of silence, until it felt like it was already happening.

And it was! I started hearing the water's giggly voice and her water droplets on my cheeks. I opened my eyes to witness the floating translucent waters gliding a couple of feet above my head.

I sat giggling as the creek broke into capillaries and engulfed the flames with her sparkly wetness.

How is this happening? Floated through the back of my mind.

Then I imagined the creek wrapping herself around the base of Eagle tree, creating a flame retardant skirt. And as if the water was directly connected to my brain, it happened! An arm of the dowsing liquid hugged the tree and sent back the flames to their nothingness.

All the fires were out!

"Yay!" yelled the crowd of chipmunks, squirrels and hawks that had gathered.

"Very good, Sara, you did that!" the hummingbird sang before she flew off.

"Thank you creek, please return," I murmured. And as a snail goes back into its shell, the water retreated to its earthly banks.

"Thank you," I said to everything and nothing in particular. I crumpled to the ground and hugged it as the air returned to my lungs. The damp fireplace smell filled the air, but the fire was out. Clem curled up beside me and put his wet nose in my ear.

"Thank you, thank you, thank you!! Whoever did that, thank you." I looked all around, shaking my head in disbelief that any of this was real.

"You did it, Sara, you did that." Eagle Tree purred.

"There's no way that was me, but thank you, Eagle Tree." I could barely mutter the words.

Then I saw it. Luckily, I'd missed it before.

There, six feet from the ground, was a large metal sign imprinted with rusted flame markings, NAILED into Eagle Tree, and etched with these words:

"GIVE ME ILANALY, SARA, OR THERE WILL BE MORE."

Sara

After the Eagle Tree fire, I let myself go to Ilanaly for their wisdom and guidance. I didn't know what to do, and Mom was no help. She couldn't turn on her own son. Even after everything he'd said and done in his 40 years, she still couldn't fathom someone she'd given birth to would do such a horrible thing. I couldn't blame her.

When I floated through the entrance, my lungs jumped for joy, taking in the deepest breath I'd taken in weeks. My body shook off the tension. The vibrant colors of the singing birds and swaying wildflowers greeted me. I was home.

The entire community was gathered in the common area, they knew I was coming before I did.

Joel slid in front of me and wrapped his arms around my shoulders, engulfing me with courage and tranquility. Everything was alright. I knew I wasn't going to get to stay with him, but his love-filled arms opened me to all the good reverberating through the air. My body twigged with the idea that I could feel this way wherever I was.

We glided over to the common area and joined the crowd. Some people sat on the grass, while others dangled from the tree branches or played in the waters that looked like they were drawn by a child, no rhyme or meaning, just flowing delight.

Joel and I sat under the tall, meandering Big Leaf Maple. My long, loose, skirt and sandals showed off my sock line and bruises from working on the farm. I felt so inelegant compared to all these ballerina figures. I leaned against Joel who was propped against the undulating gray bark of the maple. When he laid against her, her vibrating colors changed to blues and purples. The scene in Ilanaly seemed like it was constantly being painted by a masterful artist and responding to the people in the vicinity. I found I could use the tree's bark to show me how I felt. An instant biofeedback machine. Sometimes I'd touch it and it'd turn red. I was usually thinking about Brian and the fires he'd set then. But when I was with Joel, it turned greens and orange and purple, colors of new life, and divinity. Having this information helped me to feel more. Feeling the anger allowed me to feel more joy too.

Ayer, the elder of Ilanaly, was conducting the meeting, going from group to group. There was no leader, and no rules. They believed rules pushed against things and beliefs. If you focused on the good, only the good would come out.

They didn't have Brian as a brother.

Ayer began. His short white-blond hair hung in undulating rows."As you all know, we are here today to help Lily and Sara save their property and save our land," His indigo eyes sparkled with joy.

Wait, were they talking about my mom? I turned my head toward Joel.

But before I could ask, people started giving suggestions on how to protect the farm and Ilanaly from Brian's greedy fingers. It was all so orderly and considerate. There were no bad ideas. Everyone was heard and encouraged.

"That's a great idea, Shama, and we could also....." was how the conversations went.

On earth, it would've been a yelling match. There'd be at least one person in the group pushing his idea without listening to other possibilities. But here, they didn't worry, they mimicked nature and worked together for what was best for the whole. Their ideas are as intertwined as tree roots. There was no sense of lack, or entitlement, just thinking what was best for the greater good. It was refreshing and inspiring. *How could we have that on earth? What would make that possible?*

I was shaken from my meanderings when a sudden hush came over the crowd. People's faces filled with smiles as they looked in the direction of the entrance cave. I uncurled my body from between Joel's knees and gasped at the sight.

There, beaming with light, was a face I'd seen since the day I was born.

"Mom?" I barely got it out.

Ayer floated to her and embraced her, like Joel embraced me. It wasn't a friendly, quick hug. It was a long, lingering embrace, like when soldiers return from a long tour.

Sparks flew out between their bodies. *What was this about?*

I looked at Joel, "What the hell?" I don't think I'd ever cursed in Ilanaly before.

I bolted up and walked toward Mom.

"Mom! What are you doing here? Who's protecting the farm?" She and Ayer parted quickly.

"Hi, Sara. come on over here and sit with me a bit."

This couldn't be good. The only time my mom had asked me to sit next to her was to tell me my dog, Sadie, had been run over and left in the middle of our road.

"But Mom, all these people are trying to help protect the farm. Can't this wait?"

"It's okay, it's important," she said in a gentle voice that didn't seem like hers at all.

When I got to her, she took my hand, and guided me to my favorite glacier-blue waterfalls. The moss hung down between the ribbons of water, a vivid green usually reserved for painter's palettes.

We sat down on a grassy knoll where I'd spent hours hanging out with Joel, reading and just enjoying the swishing sounds. Mom took my hands. "Sara, I've left the farm to you."

"I know that, Mom. That's why Brian's so mad."

"No, Sara, I mean I've left it for good. It's yours. Me getting in the middle of you and Brian is only making things worse. I'm staying here. Mr. Stevens has transferred the title to you. It's your property now."

I pulled my hands away. "Staying here? But why? You have a whole life up there."

"Sara, I didn't tell you this before, but I first came to Ilanaly when you were only seven. I spent every day here while you kids were at school. Ayer and I fell in love. I wanted to stay then. I never wanted to leave. But it wasn't fair to you and your brothers, nor your dad."

"Why didn't you just leave Dad and all the misery he brought us?" I was raging now, shocked by the fact that I could've lived here instead of in all that hell!

"Sara, that's so complicated, and none of it matters now." Her eyes pleaded with me.

"It matters to ME! I'd much rather have lived down here than stay with that anger-filled man you call our dad! How could you have made us live through that? Especially Brian. Maybe he'd be a better person had he been loved and not beaten." I was aware of the community watching us, but I didn't care. All I could think of was how much better things could have been.

"I'm sorry, Sara. I was doing the best I could. "

"You kids never said anything about seeing the rock. As you know, Ilanaly has to come to you. I couldn't risk you kids telling everyone about Ilanaly, if I'd tried to bring you here. I had to keep it safe. Especially after your dad died, I just wanted you kids to have some sort of stability. I mean, look at what

Brian is doing now, I'm not sure it would be any different if I'd brought him here as a kid and I couldn't take that risk. Not with this place."

I felt like I was spinning in a giant ball, and my life was just twirling around me. I lowered my head for a moment realizing what all this meant. *I had to go back and make sure I protected the farm and woods from Brian. I had no choice. Ilanaly would never be safe while I was here.*

Ayer came over and gently wrapped each of our hands in his. "The community has had some great ideas. Let's go listen to them, so we can help you, Sara. You're not alone in this. You're protecting our world too."

I took a deep breath and looked over the community. Most of them I hadn't met, and yet they looked at us like we were perfection and they wanted only the best for us.

"I just feel like all this is being put on my shoulders. It doesn't feel fair." I wiped the tears from my cheeks. It was so quiet. I was embarrassed to be the center of all this attention and at the same time, so filled with love. I was a mishmash of feelings.

Mom looked at me, she was crying too. "I'm sorry Sara. I don't mean to put this all on you."

Ayer turned to me, as the singing waters swam by. "Sara, what are you really upset about?"

I looked out, and the community had returned to enjoying their world. They stayed gathered in the park, but their attention was no longer on me. Joel remained on the other side of me, while Ayer sat between Mom and me. I was so grateful for how safe I felt among these people.

I pulled my hand away from Ayer and held the thumb of my left hand, with my right fingers. "I just feel like all the blame is being put on me. I'm having to do it all by myself. And it's not fair."

Ayer's clothing looked like a monk's robe. "What are you really upset about Sara?"

I wanted to scream. I'd already answered that question. But his peace-filled eyes wouldn't let me. "Well.... um...I don't know. I feel like Brian even finding out about Ilanaly is all my fault. And I hate there's nothing I can do about it. I just wish Mom would handle him." My head dropped to my hands. "This is all too much."

Ayer soothingly rubbed my back. "Stay with me Sara, I know this sounds annoying. But what are you really upset about?"

My head bolted up and peered at Ayer. "Are you kidding me? Didn't you hear?"

Ayer's shiny white teeth showed between his lips. "Just tell me what is really bothering you about this whole thing?"

I took a deep breath and looked within. As frustrating as it was, I knew Ayer was wanting to help me. "I don't know, maybe that..... I'm not sure... that I have to take care of other things now?"

"You're doing great Sara. Stay with me. I promise this will help."

I nodded.

Ayer repeated. "What are you really upset about Sara?"

I stopped fighting the questions. Light started to seep into my closed brain. I took several deep breaths, while watching the waters tumble by, like they were bringing me the answers. I allowed their gurgles and laughs to replace my anger and frustration, they're wetness soothed my fire. *What was it? I wondered to myself. Why was I really mad about Mom staying in Ilanaly?*

The words spilled out of my mouth. "I just want to stay in Ilanaly too. There's so much I don't know yet, I've only scratched the surface. I just want Brian and the world to go away. I'm tired of earth, and now that I've found this place I want to stay here. At the same time, I know it's an escape and I've spent my life escaping. Now it's time to get in the bullpen and I'm afraid I'm going to get gored." My head fell to Joel's lap. I had nothing left.

Joel took over rubbing my back and allowed the silence to take over. Even the waters seemed to become quiet. The moments unfurled as all the possibilities drifted through my brain. *Maybe it would be better for Mom to stay here. I couldn't imagine all she'd already given up to make sure Ilanaly was safe.*

Ayer's sympathetic voice whispered. "Sara, I think the community has come up with a solution for the farm, when you're ready to hear it. I'm sorry, it will change things for you even more."

I sat up and looked at Mom, then Joel, pleading for help. My sternum tightened and my skin quaked. Mom was right, her being on the farm was making things worse with Brian. It was my turn now to do whatever it took to protect this place. I didn't want the responsibility, I'd never even had kids, but this was the answer I sought.

I nodded my head. "Okay, I'm ready." I pulled my hair back and straightened my ponytail. I stood up and reached my hand out to Joel. I was starting to feel I had support now. It wasn't just me anymore. It never was.

Sara

I don't know how long I was there lying on the dock, holding my stomach, trying to catch my breath through the sobs, but suddenly Joel was lying beside me, cradling my shivering body and kissing my head.

"What if I never get to see you again?" The tears flowed and my cells were emptying every drop of pain, every wisp of hope were all dumping themselves onto the dock and dripping into the waters below. I felt like an empty beehive full of bee corpses. I'd found the home I'd longed for, and yet I couldn't stay.

"I'm sorry, Sara, I'm so sorry." Joel held me tighter. I'd never felt so loved. It was the fuel of my courage.

I took a deep breath and turned to look at Joel. "I hate this. Do you know of other ways to get to Ilanaly?" I struggled to breathe through the pain. Joel kept holding me, breathing to the rhythm of a summer breeze, but the light was getting engulfed by darkness and I knew Joel was going to have to go soon by his translucent skin.

"Joel, go back. I can't have anything happening to you."

"I'll be back tomorrow, Sara." He pushed the hair back from my eyes. "Promise me you won't do anything until I get back."

He looked into my eyes, so innocent, but as if he knew I'd do what I wanted.

I nodded, but my fingers were crossed.

I was going to miss those soft, salty lips. I never in a million years thought I'd leave someone like Joel.

***

The next day, after all the arrangements had been made, I drove to Riley to share with people what I'd done. I wanted them to know I wasn't hurting them and their livelihood. I wanted to convince them once and for all that I wasn't crazy.

I drove through town, pondering whether to stop at the diner. It was lunchtime on a Wednesday. I pulled into a slanted parking spot a block away and studied all the familiar cars. They belonged to the guys I'd worked with for almost 20 years. I knew their families, and had watched their kids grow. The sheriff, the local banker, people who were at my baptism. I longed to connect with them, for them to accept me.

I was sitting at the counter, eating one of Ronny's giant hamburgers with all the fixin's. I'd done it hundreds of times in my life. I don't know what he put in those things. He wouldn't tell anyone, not even his wife. People came from towns over to taste those burgers.

While I was sitting there enjoying all the familiar sounds-like clanking silverware, ice hitting glass, Ronny giving Betts, his wife, a hard time, and the guys laughing, a new murmur began. I kept hearing my name from various corners.

"...she thinks trees talk...." and giggling,

"...maybe they'd walk on into my truck then....." a reply came.

"They fired her...." came a voice from another part of the diner. "Think she musta' hit 'er head or somein' out there."

"...she just went crazy...."

They thought they were whispering, but my hearing was acute. That was one result of spending years in quiet instead of around loud machinery, like most of those guys.

I pushed my plate back. I wanted to cry.

"Hey, Sara...." Suddenly standing next to me was Roper. "Hear you got your head knocked on out there." He laughed as he handed Betty a bill from his wallet.

I just stared at him. This was a guy I'd gone to school with since first grade. He'd cut a lot of the trees I marked.

Betty defended me. "Roper, you leave Sara alone now..."

As soon as Roper left, I placed a $5 bill next to my mostly full plate, pulled my baseball cap low over my eyes, and tried to walk out without anyone noticing.

Someone called out behind me, "Hey Sara, the tables talkin' to ya' too?" A bunch of guys laughed.

Another added, "yeah, maybe we hurtin' 'em by puttin' our plates on 'em!" The whole diner filled with laughter at my expense.

I swung open the glass door, ran down the street, jumped in Bessie and turned the key. Clem sat in the front seat, tongue hanging out, giving me that 'how ya' doin' look he always had. I wished for his life.

I careened home, just daring the sheriff to pull me over.

I got out next to the familiar trees surrounding the front circular drive. I walked to them and rubbed my fingers across the marks Mom had made on the elm tree. Each of us got a mark on a different tree at ages 4, 8, 12, 16-and when we graduated from high school. My tree was the chestnut grown from seeds Mema had carried across the country. Brian's was the hickory. Joey's was the elm.

The fact that we each had our own completely different species of trees was appropriate. My tree was from a completely different part of the country. They didn't normally grow here. I wondered if that was why Mom had chosen it for me. Had she somehow known?

I longed for us to be trees from the same mother tree. I'd hoped for us to be as entangled as all the trees are, imitations of the way they support each other and provide nourishment to those different from them. Always supporting the whole. My tears followed the colorful leaves to the ground. I went and sat at my favorite place along the stream. I didn't know it then, but I was saying goodbye to my lifelong friends.

I'd watched millions of gallons of water flow through this bed, always amazed that it never stopped. I was only five when I first started asking my parents about this.

"But where does it come from?" I'd ask anyone who listened. "There's just so much of it! It never stops, even when we haven't had rain or snow in months." The adults just put their hands over their face and shook their heads. They told me it came from springs in the earth, so off I'd go to find them, the places where the earth sprouted water.

"Where does all THAT water come from?" I started asking after finding a spring. "How's it possible that for centuries water just keeps coming out of the ground no matter how little or much moisture we get. It's gotta stop sometime." I don't know how I knew to ask these questions at so young an age. "There can't just be that much water sitting under the ground, I insisted." I longed for someone to explain it to me. They didn't talk about it in school.

Everyone kept brushing me off. "Oh Sara, can't you just go play with dolls like the other kids?" they would say with a sigh.

Then it occurred to me. *Maybe they didn't know where the water came from.*

It still just doesn't make sense where all this water comes from, century after century- even now that I know about all the underground waterways. Look at the Grand Canyon. Water did that! Where in the world did all that water come from? I've studied, I've pondered and nothing makes sense except that there is some Universal force of love that provides for us, that continuously gives us what we need. We are just asked to care, respect and appreciate it. The bubbling streams, like the stars, are a constant reminder of how loved we are.

As I sat with the moist ground chilling my pants, I started noticing the heartbreak and the self-hatred over how much I'd held myself back. I was ridiculed as a kid. When I could no longer take the pain, I sucked my true self deep within my skin, hidden, so no one could see. Not even me. I felt disbelief that I'd been so hard on myself. Slowly the crushing weight of fear released from my bones, swallowing up the layers I'd put over myself, ready to be released back to the earth, back to the sky, back to the place where everything is born.

The gurgling waters carried away the ache, and my lungs filled with soothing air. Blood once again pulsed through my skin after being held in tight channels against my chest for so long, only allowing the essential parts of me to receive the life-nourishing blood. Not holding on so tightly meant now I could hurt, it meant I could feel.

As a child, mostly what I felt was pain. No one cared to hear my thoughts, my questions, my disbelief in response to their canned answers. This led to me feeling there was surely something wrong with me. My own family thought I was strange. At a very young age, I curled myself into a ball, hid her deep inside, behind my sternum, inside my chest, so no one would see her, so no one would tell me I was weird, so no one would hit me and tell me to shut up. Now, all of it, all of her, came pouring out. She had to come out of the shadows, she had to have the light, she was tired of being locked in the dark caves of her mind and soul.

When the sun started to fall behind the hills I got up and brushed off my jeans.

"Whoooo Hoooo!" I yelled, as if I was riding a roller coaster. I wrapped my arms around the tree I'd been leaning against and let her love and compassion flow into my veins. I held her smooth gray bark as if I would take her into my body.

Clem whined, bringing me out of my trance.

I didn't want to leave the land I knew so well. I felt I needed to stay and protect her, make sure no one hurt Mother Tree and all her children. Make sure no one killed the rabbit family that's lived under our front porch for as long as I've been alive. I wanted to make sure no one tainted her waters or found the entrance to Ilanaly. The Nature Conservatorship I set up was supposed to protect her, even from Brian, but I felt like if I wasn't there, no one would truly go to the lengths to save her that I would.

And yet I knew I needed to go. It was time for me to see what else was out there. My home would always be here when I wanted to come back. I hoped.

I felt a rope was connected from my heart to Wonder Tree, a rope that wouldn't let me get in the truck and go. *One more night*, I thought to myself, *I'll stay just one more night.*

But Wonder Tree disagreed. "Go, I'll be with you no matter where you are. Our bond will never break."

As the tears that welled up in my eyes fell around my nose and across my lips, I hopped in the truck and left. Left a lifetime of memories, good and bad, left my best friends, the ones who got me through the roughest of days.

"You can talk to us from anywhere, Sara, we're always here," whispered the voices as my view of my old world faded away.

***

I drove late into the night following an inner tug.

The next morning, Clem and I woke up to a new scene.

I realized this was the first day of my new life. Have you ever felt freedom and excitement about what's in front of you but also sadness over what you left behind? That's how I felt.

I was alone and yet comfortable and safe. I felt the possibilities of the open road, I had nowhere to be and no one to be responsible for except Clem and myself.

I enjoyed the flourishing sense of stillness and love, like I did in Ilanaly.

The only tree I saw was 100 yards away, and it was struggling to be a tree. All I saw for miles was tanned dirt, laid flat.

After spending my entire life among the thick forests of the Northwest, I felt like I'd entered a ghost town-except there was no town.

The quiet here seemed much different than in the woods. More complete. No rushing water, or bird songs. No crackling branches from critters' adventures.

It sank into my soul and settled there. It was even hard to move, as I didn't want to break the silence. Every move I made felt like I was betraying a trust, disturbing a sanctuary, like talking in church.

I got out my backpacking stove and set it on a rock to heat up some water for my morning tea. Here the ground was so barren I didn't feel I needed to raise my stove above the plants. I did anyway, still concerned about starting a wildfire.

As I sipped my warming tea, the sun began to rise above a dirt sea with only islands of rocks to block its path to me.

I heard a hum. It didn't feel mechanical, or man-made, it felt natural, like the dirt was singing a baby's babble.

I held still for a few minutes and the hum became more pronounced and relaxing. I was being serenaded by the grandest of choirs.

I had heard something similar when I was in the Washington woods by myself and away from streams and bird songs. But there the tone was a little different, a little more high pitched, and a little weaker.

Here the sound was intense and pronounced, as there was nothing holding it back, nothing to compete with, nothing to dampen its voice.

Chills ran across my skin and I felt so much appreciation for the gift of the song, the views, the emptiness.

I started hearing my mema's voice in the hum. Her spirit started penetrating my skin and bones. I heard the stories she told, and the adventures she had, which filled me with courage. Hearing this melody, leaving space for the quiet voices that want to remind me of my true nature, is one of the many reasons I love being on my own, especially in the woods. When I'm awash with people's chatter and noisy machines, I don't hear the nudges, the guidance from the other side. I wished I felt this same joy and peace with people, but I didn't. People equaled pain.

With the humming backdrop, I asked myself why I enjoyed my time in the woods. *What was it I enjoyed?*

The words trickled out on the paper, and they surprised me as they came to life.

"No one expects anything of me in the woods. I get to just be myself. No one is telling me I should do this or that, or wear this thing to look like a girl. The trees don't care, they keep to themselves. The animals don't care as long as you don't threaten them. In the woods everything just is, is allowed to be, it's only humans that need to tell a tree how to grow with our pruning shears, or an animal how to behave because they created a hole in 'our' yard.

"People just don't seem to be capable of letting others be who they are without judgment or concern. Everyone seems to think 'I'm right and you're wrong.' There's so much fighting and condemnation over how people are living their lives."

"Even I do it about people who kill animals solely for the 'fun' of it, or to show off to their friends. As well as people who drive over plants, so they can get to the perfect spot, rather than just getting out and walking."

"Because the wilderness doesn't judge me, or expect me to be different, I'm protective of her. I know not everyone can hear the animals and trees like me, and maybe that makes the difference."

As the words rolled around in my mind and into my notebook, I suddenly caught a flash of bumpy brown and tan moving towards me. I moved my eyes toward the motion, while keeping the rest of my body still, and there, only 5 feet from me was a lone toad hopping ever so reluctantly across the desert floor. She hopped like she knew where she was going and was concerned I was going to keep her from getting there.

"It's okay toad friend, I won't hurt you. You're safe." The tears welled up in my eyes as I broke the silence and felt so much love for this unexpected creature.

I wished so much I felt the same for other people. I wanted to feel a connection to someone other than Joel. But every time I tried, I was betrayed, teased-or worse, kept in a box, to keep me from changing. It was exhausting and heartbreaking. Maybe I tried to be friends with the wrong people. Maybe I wasn't picky enough.

I couldn't imagine how the toad survived in such harsh conditions. Toads still need water to produce their offspring, even if they didn't need it to proceed with life. *If he could thrive when the odds were against him, why couldn't I?*

The toad heard me and moved on towards the south.

It left me with my anger and tears. *Why couldn't I make friends? Why did people have to be so mean?*

Why did they have to torment me because I saw things differently than they did? What were they afraid of? Why wasn't it okay for us to think differently? Why was I dubbed crazy, because I suggested to people that maybe there was more to the trees and animals than they could see.

I couldn't believe that God created all these fantastic creatures just so they could hang on our walls.

I wanted to feel safe at home. I wanted to feel as loved and respected around people as I did out here in the middle of nowhere. I just didn't know how.

Maybe this trip would lead me to figuring it out.

I wasn't certain it was possible to feel around people the way I did out here, but I became open to the possibility I'd find my home, people who understood me. I found it in Ilanaly. Maybe it existed on earth too.

The sun was above the horizon and there was nothing left in my cup but a tea bag. It was time for me to be on my way.

I packed up my things, got Clem in the car after pulling cactus needles from his nose, then put my keys in the ignition.

Before I could hear the roar of Bessie, Clem started yapping and jumping in the seat. I looked up and a cloud- literally a *cloud*-of butterflies, was right outside my windshield. What moments ago was open air was now filled with a cacophony of fluttering orange and blacks. The air sounding like a child whispering radio static.

Clem hushed, and we sat gaped at the thousands of butterflies circling our truck. Laughter leapt out of my mouth uncontrollably as the joy tears streamed down my cheeks. I so wanted to get out and be engulfed with the colored tissue-papered creatures but feared I'd hurt them. I closed my eyes and just let the sound fill my cells.

"You can help us, Sara, you can save us," I heard them call to me. Their words buoyed me and I knew they were right. They, the trees, the frogs, I was here to help them in whatever way I could.

"You're okay, you're perfect as you are, you don't have to change or do anything different," they continued. "Thank you for hearing us."

A power rose up in my belly, a beam of light filled with confidence.

Maybe there were other ways to get to Ilanaly.

Maxine

"Mom! I'm not coming home. I need to do this." I spoke into the black plastic receiver.

"Okay, Max, but it sounds like you're on a wild goose chase looking for this Sara. You haven't got a clue where to look for her or even if she's still alive. You need to save your money and look for a job. You'll figure it out from there." Her voice sounded gargled and hissed in the hard black receiver.

"Mom, please understand." I wanted to sit down, but the stiff metal cord wouldn't reach the ground.

"I do, Max, I just want to make sure you have a nest egg. I want you to have enough." It was like I was talking to a different mom. She'd been so supportive of me leaving initially. It baffled me why she wanted me home now.

"Hey girly, get outta' there! Go home and let us adults use the phone!"

A wrinkled, white-haired man stared at me through the glass of the phone booth. I scanned his belongings to see if there was any sign of a gun, but all I saw was the top of a whiskey bottle. The man's stubble was turning into a beard, and his clothes had been through a war.

"Just a minute. I'm almost done." I spoke in his direction, taking my mouth away from the receiver.

"Max, why didn't you call on your cell phone?"

"Mom, it's expensive. I don't want you paying for that." I wanted to be independent. I was 22 years old. Having my mother pay for things felt icky.

"Well, it doesn't sound safe where you are, get out of there and call me back on your cell phone." Her voice rose like it did when I was five and she found me near the bread cutting machine at the co-op.

"Mom, it's just a drunk old man. He won't hurt me."

"How do you know?" Her voice teetered on a shout.

"I just do." I whispered.

BANG! BANG BANG!! The whole booth shook, and the glass shaken to the edge of its limits. "I said get out of there! I need to use the phone now or my wife is gonna leave me." The white-haired man shouted as loud as his scratchy voice could.

Somehow, I doubted he had a wife on the other end of a phone line.

"I'll be done in just a minute, sir."

"NOW." He pounded again. "I said get out of there now. What you doin' without your mamma anyhow? You need' get on home."

Was this some kind of sign from the universe telling me to give up on this journey and go home? I'd only been out for one month, and I'd planned for two more. I was feeling hopeless as I kept following the urges and having some great experiences, but none of them led me one step closer to finding Sara. *Maybe they were right.*

"Max? Max, you still there?" said Mom's voice, now shouting.

I felt like I was at some kind of carnival. After a month in the quiet woods, all the sounds were piercing my brain.

"Yes, Mom. I'm not coming home, okay? I really need to do this." I tried to sound convincing. It was so hard saying that to the woman who'd worked so hard to send me to college and give me a nice place to live. I wanted to please her and make her proud, make her know all the effort she put in wasn't wasted. *Was she right? Was it time to go home?*

"Fine, but please call more often. A month is too long."

BANG! "I said gi' out now!" The man seemed to stand up only through sheer will.

"I will, Mom, I better go. Love you."

"Love you too, Max, be safe out there." Her voice had softened into a lullaby.

"I am." I reluctantly put the receiver back on the silver box. *Not sure if I was telling the truth or not.*

I turned to the noisy man. "Hey, I'm coming out now. Stand back and give me some room, okay?"

"No little kid is gonna tell me what to do. You get out there now." He banged against the metal of the booth.

I'd had lots of experience dealing with upset customers when I was working the check-outs at the coop, I tried to call up some of that confidence now. It seemed people really just wanted to be heard.

I slowly opened the folding doors just barely enough to get my bony body through the door. As soon as my limbs were free, I ran toward Pearl, jumped in and locked the doors.

The old man fiddled around with the booth trying to figure out how to open the doors. He pulled and pushed and shook them until he collapsed against the side of the phone booth and went to sleep. I wanted to help him, but my gut told me to stay put.

Help me please, I said with my heart. *I really need your guidance right now. Do I go home?*

Silence.

Knowing I needed to at least find a place to sleep for the night, I pulled my Benchmark map from under my cooler on the passenger seat. I was in Roseburg, Oregon now. North seemed like the most logical choice, but did I go up Interstate 5 to Portland or head out to the coast? Unfortunately, I-5 seemed like the right choice. Sometimes this following your intuition stuff is really hard and I just wanted to take back control and do things my own way. But, still, it's been so much more fun seeing where things go and following my heart to places I'd never been.

But really, Interstate 5? I hate interstates.

$\mathcal{S}$ara

With an army of nature conservationists caring for the property, and thanks to Mom's investments, I was free to do whatever I wanted, and yet I didn't feel free. I still felt something was holding me down. I knew the best way to feel space in my brain was to walk.

I really didn't know where I was going. I was just driving south through Eastern Oregon when I saw a big sign-*Pacific Crest Trail*. I'd heard about people spending months walking it. I swerved over and parked at the trailhead. I grabbed my pack, a couple liters of water, a sleeping bag, and a bag of M and M's-because you can't have a good walk without chocolate-and threw them in my pack. Clem had his own pack filled with his food and water. When I put that pack on him, he could barely hold still.

The September light was quickly turning to dark, so I took off down the trail towards the California border and have been walking ever since. That was 5 days ago. Every step I took away from Joel chipped away at my heart.

Seemed most of the people were headed north. They were all friendly. Some people wore headphones, many people hiked in groups. The dense evergreen forests south of Crater

Lake opened into dry lands pockmarked with treeless ponds, then took us back into rocky, green mountains once in California.

The trail was busy enough that it didn't feel like my weeks in the woods when I worked for the Dittons. I missed the solitude of those days. And what was worse was the amount of trash and toilet paper some hikers left. I didn't understand why someone would belittle such beauty and leave a pile of toilet paper at the foot of a lovely tree. It was definitely the minority of people backpacking, but one pile of white under a redwood was more than I wanted to see.

On the seventh day, almost in mid-stride, I got the urge to return to my car. I hadn't had any life-changing revelations, but the inner waters had calmed.

September made eating in northern California mountains a little more challenging than when I had hiked during the summer berry season. There were still rose hips and dandelion greens. Luckily the first frost hadn't hit yet. But the woods always provide. You just gotta know where to look.

I'll be honest, I kept thinking about the steak and pie I was gonna have when I got back to town. Every person who's spent days in the woods knows that feeling of just wanting something filled with nothing but calories.

***

On the 3rd day back to my truck, I noticed a haze surrounding the base of Mt. Hood, northwest of me. It was another cloudless day, and all the plants were calling out for rain. I had come out of the mountains and was crossing the lowlands back into southern Oregon. It was hard to see it until I got into the open lands. It wasn't the white clouds that covered the top. It was like dirt was trying to make its way up the mountain. Was it smog from Portland?

I kept moving on and decided I'd find out at the next watering hole. I suspected, but I had to be sure.

I didn't even make it to the outpost before my worst fears were confirmed by a group of young hikers heading south. Wildfire. Where, they weren't sure. Southern Washington. But the PCT wasn't affected. The group continued on and left me with my anger.

I didn't want to hear anymore. I didn't care. I couldn't care. I couldn't spend my life trying to protect the world from my brother. It might not even be him.

My gut told me differently.

The next day five young thru-hikers started passing me on the trail going northbound.

"You may want to hurry if you intend to make it past that fire before they close the trail down," said the tallest girl of the group. Her green baseball cap was almost brown, her tanned legs slid out the bottom of her shorts, and her smile was that of the happiest person on earth.

"What! I thought the fire wasn't anywhere near the trail."

"This is a new one that's started, it's near Crater Lakes," said the young man standing next to her. They waved and continued on.

It was like my brother knew where I was and was making sure I was miserable. *There's no way he could know where I am.* I thought to myself. I shook my head, as if shaking off a pesky fly, and kept heading back to my car, still three long days of hiking away.

Thoughts started seeping in. *What should I do when I get back to my car? Should I try to help? Try to find Brian and stop him? How many more fires would he start?*

"Wait a minute," I said out loud to nothing. "I'm making a big assumption. This may just be wildfires. People leave warm campfires all the time, not realizing how easy it is to start a fire in these dry woods. I can't keep blaming Brian every time there's a fire." I bit my lip, wanting to believe what I was saying. My stomach clinched, as if to hold in the truth. I knew but I didn't want to know. I wanted to get on with my life. And I REALLY didn't want to go back to a place where I was considered a whack job.

Out here, nobody cares if I talk to trees, I thought. *They all get the joy of sleeping on the earth every night.*

The trees whispered to me gently, "Sara, you know it's him." There was less vegetation surrounding the trees here. It was mostly ground dotted by ponderosa trees and mountain mahogany. Something about being able to see further than the brambled woods of the northwest, was freeing.

"NO, NO, NO, NO, NO! I don't care! What the fuck?" I shouted. " Why am I always the one who has to take care of things? Why is this my responsibility? It's not, it's Mom's! She raised the sick fiend, why doesn't SHE take care of it? Isn't it enough that I left Ilanaly and the farm?" My hands were covering my ears the whole time-as if that was going to stop me from hearing them.

The trees continued to murmur. "Sara, only you can stop this. You've seen the visions of what could happen. The devastation to thousands of lives, and Ilanaly."

"PLEASE! I can't do this. I just can't. I'm so tired. So tired of being the butt of jokes, of being made fun of for talking with you trees. First of all, I don't know HOW I could stop such enormous fires, and second, even if I DID, then EVERYONE will know what I can do and the entire country will be gawking at me. I'll never be able to go anywhere. I'll never get away from all the HATE and MEANNESS! I just want it to stop! I just want FAR away from the torture." I kicked the earth like it was causing the pain until my shame-filled body gave out and collapsed in the dusty dirt.

But then I felt a presence around me. Not the sort of ethereal presence I was used to when birds visited me. It was more solid and familiar.

I looked up and there looking back at me was 5 pairs of compassionate eyes shining on me.

A tanned brown-haired girl kneeled down, touched my elbow, and looked into my eyes. "Are you okay? Is there anything we can do?"

The sympathy in her eyes was overwhelming. I'd never seen a person show so much love and compassion. I threw my arms around her and sobbed.

The whole group put their arms around me. Not a word was spoken. I just felt love seeping from their pores, like I'd felt so many times coming from the trees. This group of strangers took me under their wing. Their hearts started pumping in unison, and I felt so loved. I didn't know people could care this much. I just kept crying, and they kept holding me, like they had no better place they'd rather be.

"Thank you," I finally whispered through my tear-covered lips.

They gave me a squeeze.

I didn't understand. I was so confused. How could these absolute strangers who just witnessed a crazy woman screaming into the air have so much love and compassion? I'd never felt anything like this except from Joel and the trees.

"Who are you?" Tears gargled my whisper.

I took a deep inhale, a second smaller one and exhaled. They held their embrace, and I took another deep breath. The relaxing kind, when you can feel all the tears have been shed, and a sense of peace and quiet inhabits your pain-filled body. A meadow full of wildflowers consumed my soul.

I didn't know what it was about a good cry that could bring such a profound sense of space and stillness.

The group released their embrace and sat beside me.

"Do you want to walk with us? Nothing like a good walk to help figure things out." I stared at the dirty blond (literally) boy who said that. It was like he was telling me what I always said to myself.

"No thank you," I sniffled. "I don't want to hold you back." I wiped my face and stared at the ground.

"We've got all day and everything we need on our backs." The boy put his hand on my left shoulder and the girl put a hand on my right shoulder. "If it helps, we'd love to walk with you."

I'd been out on the PCT for 10 days, and these were the first people I'd really talked to. These people, these strangers who just happened by when I was yelling out my pain seemed to understand, to get it. *Why?*

***

A day later, for the first time in my life, I found myself walking with a group of people, and enjoying it. Few words were said, even when we stopped to sleep. We all woke a little before the sun, gathered our things, and kept going. There was a familiarity with them that I couldn't voice. They looked like all the other thru-hikers going by, but the way they moved, their energy wasn't as substantial. They almost glowed.

It intrigued them that I'd only brought M & Ms (which were running scarily low). So I showed them some plants and barks they could eat and they loved it! It felt more satisfying than their freeze-dried meals.

There's something about eating from the earth when you're in the woods that just seems right. I'm lucky though, I've spent a lifetime learning about plants, what's good and what's deadly.

These former strangers even walked the same pace I did. No one complained that I walked too fast and said that I should slow down for them. We all happily trooped along. I was so comfortable with this group of people who needed so few words. It was like we were getting to know each other at a cellular level. Our DNA was talking, so we didn't have to.

I don't know if I was blocking out the tree's voices, or they were giving me space. It would be just like them not to push, and let me find my path.

It was the second day of my group hike, with only one day left to my car. We were returning to the higher hills dominated by fir trees in Southern Oregon. Clouds had moved in during the night and refused to release their hold. They'd heard the plants pleas and gave us all a much needed shower. As we trotted along the winding trail, I was lost in the miracle of finding compatible people. I'd found I enjoyed having people to listen to the bird songs with, and wonder what bird it was. The birds were starting to migrate, so I saw some feathered friends. I'd found pleasure in watching the sun settle through the stands of Ponderosa Pine with others who were mesmerized too. It was baffling that I felt so comfortable. The only other people I'd felt this comfortable with were people in Ilanaly.

A flash went through my mind. No, it can't be-they can't breathe here.

Then I remembered what the trees had asked me to do.

"FUCCKKK!"

Everyone stopped and looked at me. That's when I realized I'd said it out loud. My dirt-covered skin kept peeking out from under my poncho.

"Sorry guys." I lowered my eyes.

"No worries. It's a good word when no other word will do," said Hale, who'd only spoken a couple of words during our two days together. She beamed at me with a knowing smile. A group of hikers waved as they passed by us.

We grinned. "I was told I said it way too much, especially for a girl. But I think it was the first word I heard from my dad when I popped out of the womb."

We gathered in a small circle. I looked at their faces. "I've got a big decision to make, and I'll be back to my car tomorrow. When I get there, I've got to make a choice, and I just don't know if I can do it." I shook my head and bit my lip. I didn't want to leave the trail. The safety of just taking one step at a time and breathing the soily air.

Hale smiled, "Can we help? We're not expert choice makers, mind you, but sometimes it feels good just to talk out loud."

Chris, the blond haired boy chuckled, "other than to the trees."

We all laughed, remembering the day they found me. I felt so close to these people. People I didn't even know existed three days ago. I didn't know if it was the walking, the woods, or the universe just sending them to me when I needed them, that made them feel like people I'd known for years. It was a welcome change to the solitary life I lived.

"Okay guys, this is gonna sound crazy, but somehow I know you'll get it."

Karen, the brown-haired girl who was the first to embrace me that day, nodded in agreement.

We all sat down under one of the bigger Ponderosa Pines whose bark smelled like butterscotch and looked like it was blushing. It was as if he was saying to us as he patted his trunk, "come, come sit here." They usually drop their lower branches as they grow so they make a great sitting-under tree.

I jumped off the deep end. "I can talk to trees, and the best part is-they talk to me."

Nothing, not a word or even startled look. A chickadee did its 'everything is alright' call from a branch high above.

"And those wildfires ahead of us, I think they were started by my brother. He's mad at me, and he's killing the things I care about most." I stared into each of their eyes, hoping for understanding.

"That sucks." Chris consoled me.

My shoulders dropped. I was sharing my darkest secret and being heard, not mocked. "I won't go into all the details of why, BUT the trees tell me I can put out the fires. That's what they said when you found me, when I was telling them NO, I wasn't going. And now the fires have raged on and I've done nothing but walk out here with you guys." I shook my head, feeling disgusted at myself. I'd let those I cared about down.

"So you can put out fires people can't?" Hale's eyes were wide.

"Yes, at least, I put out a smaller one. Turns out not only can I talk to trees, but the water and animals do what I want." I was talking barely above a whisper, looking over my shoulders, afraid of the scoldings to come.

"Sara! That is so cool. I wish I could do that. There's been some days I wished a pond would just pour itself all over me!" Chris threw his arms in the air and looked up like he could see a pond pouring water over his head.

No judgment, just awe. Here I'd been hiding all along, thinking no one would understand since the people in my town didn't, and these friendly strangers were impressed, not threatened by my abilities. A raven cawed in the background, like he was telling all his friends my good news.

Karen asked innocently. "So, Sara, what's the decision? Why are you still here and not there putting out the fires?"

And there it was. It hit me like a falling tree. Why was I still here when I could save thousands of trees and hundreds of lives? I was stunned. They made it sound so simple, like the easiest question in the world to answer.

I felt *dumb* and *numb*.

They looked at me, eyebrows up, calmly smiling, like they couldn't wait to hear the answer. They really wanted to understand what I felt.

I had no words, just a tightness in my chest. I was holding something in. Something that had been inside me for so long, it'd taken root in my lungs and stomach. It was part of me. Like I was born with it.

But I wasn't. It wasn't even friendly. It was there to keep me safe. Safe from others' words and thoughts.

And what did that matter now? How was it helping? What was the problem with others' thoughts and words, they were just a reflection of them. I'd felt scared many times over, and I walked right through it. But this, this strangling vine, had taken me hostage, made me one of its own, coursed through my blood and veins, making me think it was real.

Was it?

Did it matter? What would happen if I tore it loose, threw it in a deep, deep hole where it could never trap anyone again?

Ohh, the thought of that felt scary, empty, spaceless. *What would I do? Who would I be without that clinging life form that was merely a belief? How would I act? Where would I go?*

I didn't know.

My chest started trembling, like some inner earthquake was taking shape. Two opposing forces fighting a duel.

I looked at my new friends. They were all glowing. "Sara, we're here for you." I heard them say, though no one's lips moved.

The inner shaking got stronger and stronger. A fracture in the hardened surface began to allow space and light between the form and my sternum. Slowly, one by one, the form's hold was plucked from each rib, inching towards my throat.

No! I thought. *No! I don't know what to do without it.* I squeezed my rib cage, trying to tame the release. *I don't think I can stand the fear, the emptiness, the unknown!* My thoughts were trying to stop what my body and soul had already decided to do.

My companion's eyes were holding me, telling me it was okay. I saw Joel's eyes in theirs.

There was no stopping the ripping happening in my chest. Bit by bit, I started being able to breathe deeper, steadier. The inner shakiness that was a daily friend started to lessen until the dark form only had roots in my diaphragm and Adam's apple.

I heard in the breeze. "Do it, Sara, take the step now. It's your turn. You can let the rest of this go."

I could see it now as the belief form was separating from me. The fear of what others thought was such a part of me, I could even taste it. I'd made it real. Like their words could hurt me. Like anyone could truly hurt me.

"That's right Sara, you're endless, they can't hurt you, they never could.," continued the lumbering pine.

But the sting of hateful words felt so real. Like it would knock the life out of me. I never wanted to feel that pain again.

The Ponderosa Pine continued to whisper. "So you created this armor, didn't you, Sara? A shroud you thought would keep you safe. Instead, it just dampened the pain and hid the real you."

Suddenly, an impulse overtook me. I quickly got up and started digging a hole with my cat-hole trowel. And as if on cue, like they'd heard my inner thoughts, my new friends got out their trowels and started digging, too. No questions, just helping their companion.

When the hole looked like a human could fit in it, I crawled inside and screamed. "AAARRRRRR!!!!!" A primal sound came out of my belly, a sound that felt like it'd been waiting for decades to leave, to be let out of its cave.

I put my hands on my Adam's apple and belly button and pulled the imaginary being from my body, threw it in the hole, jumped out and rapidly started covering it up, one trowel of dirt at a time. My friends didn't help. They knew this part I had to do alone.

After the hole was filled and the being covered, my body rag-dolled, a lifeless mass, but shiny and new. No more running. No more tension in my body. The pain I tried to avoid, the fear of what others would think. I couldn't do it anymore. It exhausted me trying to be someone they liked-having to keep hidden so as to feel good about myself.

I WAS DONE!! No fucking more! Those people couldn't take my life from me. They couldn't take the things I loved. *And they sure as hell weren't going to take Ilanaly.*

To hell with what they thought about me. I WAS ENOUGH! I MATTERED! SOMEONE CARED ABOUT ME! AND I WAS LOVED!

The words careened through my body, replacing the fear, hurt and emptiness.

I slumped to the ground, feeling the earth take hold of my body, instill new roots, and awaken the sinews and cells that had been asleep for so long. The strands of my DNA that had been asleep since my mema died, came alive. My body once again contained the wisdom of a woman who looked at fear and kept walking. A woman who didn't take crap from anyone. Her memories, her ways filled the emptiness where fear and pain once resided. Now only I remained, free of the cruel words of everyone else.

Maxine

I don't know why I ever doubt Polly. (Polly is what I have come to call that nebulous sound I hear that seems to guide me on these adventures. It's not really a female voice, but the name reminds me of a Parrot and sometimes I feel the voice is just echoing me, getting me to hear the obvious.)

What a day! I'm now camped just outside an area that burned from a human-caused wildfire only months ago. I overheard a ranger and a gas station clerk talking about a woman who's been hanging around in the area. Wherever she goes, the plants seem to thrive.

So.... I'm thinking it may be Sara! Right? I was guided up on this horrible interstate for some reason. I'm really not sure where I am, but I went over the Columbia River so at least I know I'm in Washington.

It was a painful night. My mom's voice kept replaying in my mind. "Come home, Max! You're wasting your money."

I feel like I'm betraying her, letting her down after all she's done. I thought she was okay with this journey. I wonder what happened. Does she know something I don't?

I ended up camping in a parking lot stuck between a hotel and restaurant last night, just shortly after I went over the river.

People kept coming out talking like they were still in the bar, and it woke me up periodically. Plus I hated those awful bright lights that keep people from seeing the dark. About 2 am I got up and drove some more, slowly this time, making sure I was going the right way. Having to drive so fast on interstates, it's hard for me to know that I'm following my inner guidance. I still wasn't sure when I crossed over the river. I didn't think I'd go most of the way through Oregon in one day.

So here I was crawling down the highway with the occasional truck going by, and I needed some caffeine badly. I pulled into a Love's truck stop. Whoever came up with that name is an excellent marketer! I have a choice between all these gas stations and, ya know, Love's just seems like the ideal choice.

Going to these places after being in the woods can be shocking and unsettling. It sets my nervous system to full throttle. The music, and insanely bright lights feel jarring from the quietness and natural lighting of the woods. It feels like it keeps me from hearing and seeing what's real. I'm not sure why people need such lighting, but no one asked me.

I tried to get some gas, but the pump wouldn't take my card. I went to a couple of the gas pumps and none of them would work, so it forced me to go inside. I don't know why I keep doubting that something good's gonna come from these inconveniences, when I'm led a different way than I intended, but I still do. I cursed at the pump under my breath all the way to the door. It was about 7 am; there were guys with reflective vests filling their thermos with coffee and grabbing bags of donuts, and there were guys in Carhartts and t-shirts picking out Red Bull's and Cokes. Then there at the cash register was a leaf-green uniformed forest ranger from the local national forest. I couldn't see which one. I was eager to get out of there, but then I heard the word 'fire', so slowly I inched closer to hear the conversation.

"Yeah, it's a shame what happened to the ole' Miller place. Been there 100 years with no problems until someone comes along and has a campfire during a drought. I don't know why these people insist on these fires when it's 90 degrees outside." The cashier shook his head and slowly punched in numbers on the cash register. "There's signs all over saying no fires. I bet they were up and gone before those first sparks hit the forest floor."

"Yep." The ranger nodded as he took sips from his coffee mug and handed the cashier a twenty.

The cashier was holding the bill, waving it around. He seemed unaware of the line forming behind me. "Yeah, I do wonder that. But it's been amazing to watch the plants coming back in certain areas. What's up with that anyway? Never seen such a thing."

"It's that woman that everyone is calling a witch," the ranger said, taking another sip from his coffee mug. "We've tried to get her out of that area, just doesn't seem safe. Those torched trees just fall right over with these winds. But she disappears, just when I think I'm getting close." He shook his head and put down the mug. They still seemed oblivious to the anxious workers behind me. "Can't find a vehicle of any type. I have to say, it seems she's doing some good, so I'm not too annoyed- just don't want her to get hurt." The ranger turned around and glanced at me as I strained to listen.

"Let's just hope she can disappear under a falling tree!" The cashier replied as he finally put the money in the till. They chuckled, and the cashier handed the ranger his receipt. The ranger tipped his hat and headed for the door.

I wanted to catch up to the ranger, so I bounced out of line and left my coffee on the counter. "Sir! Sir!" I called softly to the ranger.

He didn't turn around.

I ran up and got in front of him. He jolted to a stop and his puzzled look made me realize he hadn't heard my calls. I just hoped he wouldn't pull out his gun.

"Can I help you, young lady?" he said professionally.

"Yes, yes..... I'm sorry to bother you." I was still trying to keep my voice from getting too loud.

We walked through the double glass doors of the building into the horizontal rays of sun outside. Made me feel like I'd been up all night, just seeing the sun after all those hours of driving.

"What can I do for you?" He stopped and took another drink of his coffee.

I quivered. "Um..." I took a deep breath, something about talking to authority figures frightened me. "I, I... um.... heard you talk about a woman..... in the burned area. I, um...wondered if you would tell me where that is." I tried to smile.

"You need to stay out of there, young lady. It's not safe. We have all the roads closed. If we catch you in there, you'll get fined, or worse, arrested." His voice had gone from friendly to imposing.

"I understand. I just need to find the woman you were talking about," I pleaded.

He chuckled. "Yeah, well, good luck with that. We've been trying to catch her for a month. You listen to me, you need to stay outta' that burned area. It's closed and it's illegal for anyone to be in there. It's for your safety." He raised his eyebrows and looked straight into my eyes.

I feigned helplessness. "Well, that'll be easy. I don't even know where it is."

"Good." He nodded, tipped his hat, walked to his green chevy pickup and got in. Didn't even glance my way again.

"Argh!! What should I do?" I said, barely audible even to myself.

Mom'll come drag me back home if I get arrested! I shook my head, wishing it was easier. *I have to see if that woman is Sara.* I decided silently. I got back to Pearl and sat contemplating my next move. *First, I have to figure out where that burn area is around here.* I thought to myself. *Can't be far, right?*

I went back inside the market to get my coffee. The song "Jeremiah was a Bullfrog" was blaring over the loudspeakers. I snickered. That's how I feel about Polly. Only my good friend sounds like an invisible parrot. *Now what Polly?*

I grabbed my coffee, handed the cashier two singles, and walked out the glass doors. *You got me this far, though I fought you every step of the way. You've hooked me. Now lead me the rest of the way.*

***

Sadly, it turns out there's lots of burned forest around here.

I came across one area that looked newer than the others up Highway 158. I noticed several places that had some greenery growing in them already, so I was pretty certain that the woman was in the vicinity.

I waited until dusk and walked up a trail just outside the burned area. I really didn't want to break any laws. Well, I've broken some rules, but I respect the Forest Service and understand what they're trying to do. So I was hoping maybe I could get a glimpse of the area if I hiked above it. So much easier if I were a crow! Man, those things have aerobatic ingenuity. They twist and twirl and flitter about-just playing with their best friend, the wind.

I carried my flashlight, a sleeping bag, light coat, a couple of liters of water and a little food. I was prepared to be out for the night. If I'd known what was going to happen, I'd have brought more.

I really don't know why I wasn't scared. Here I was for the first time in my life, preparing to sleep out in the woods by myself without Pearl's safety nearby. I guess I had a focus, a purpose-and that made it alright.

I hiked well past dark. Not something I'd ever done, nor something I'd recommend. Every little change in the ground is a tripping hazard. I felt like I'd just drunk a bottle of whiskey! It was slow going and the quiet was chilling. No birds, no crackling of distant animals running through the forest. The place felt abandoned-only the ghosts of the lost lives hovering about. Let's hope the person who started this fire doesn't show up in the woods again. They may have some pant-wetting experiences!

I came upon a flat area after steadily climbing for a few hours, so it felt like a good place to stop. Trees that had narrowly escaped the torture surrounded me. This was going to be a good place to watch and see if I saw any lights from the mysterious woman wandering around.

I only had granola bars for dinner, but I wasn't that hungry anyway. I picked away at my bar and looked into the dark, occasionally peering up at my friends glistening in the night sky.

Occasionally, I'd hear a stick break or some rocks move, but nothing that seemed inordinately out of place. That's why her presence was so shocking.

Where had she come from? How did she just appear? Was I making this all up?

"You looking for me, they say." A gray-haired woman stood above me, wearing an ankle-length brown skirt, flannel shirt and running shoes. The nimble woman sat down and looked out over the surrounding hills. Her lips were creased in a horizontal line. There were wrinkles all across her face, around her lips and the sides of her eyes, but her cheeks were smooth.

Her braided hair had been bleached by the sun making it cloud color.

"Who?"

"Why you lookin' for me?" She continued, ignoring my question.

I was trembling. *Who or what was I talking to?* Was this person really here? Do I run?

"I'm not sure I am looking for you. Who are you?" I tried to sound brave.

"That's none of your business. Why you here? What you lookin' at?" Her voice was firm and mesmerizing.

There was something in her eyes that told me she would not hurt me. I didn't know who she was, but her eyes were filled with both gentleness and pain. She had no interest in inflicting it on someone else.

"I'm Maxine." I reached out my hand to her, but she just kept looking me in the eye. Questioning me, like somehow my innards were going to answer her.

There was no hiding from her. She saw all of me, even with nothing but the starlight. She'd get her answers whether or not I spoke them.

"Have one?" She nodded toward my granola bars.

"Of course." I handed her one and noticed her hands. *Her hands looked older than the 54 Sara would be right now, but who knows what living in the woods does to someone?*

We sat like two friends, staring at the stars, absorbing their light.

After she finished her bar, I offered her some water, which she waved away. "Not good," she mumbled.

I didn't know if she meant the granola bar, the water, or me.

She laid back like she was in my living room and we'd known each other our whole lives. My eyes had told her what she needed to know, but my questions remained unanswered.

"Um, would you mind telling me who you are?" I tried to sound sure.

"Yes." she said in a barely audible voice.

It had to be Sara, right?! She had to know I'd found her notebook and was looking for her. That's what she saw in my eyes, right?

"Okay. Well, if you want to stay here, I can set up my tent." My stomach was turning circles, but my instincts told me it was all right.

"I'll sleep right here." She kept staring at the stars.

Now setting up my tent just felt foolish and wimpy. Unlike my neighbor, I got out my sleeping bag and pad. She just slept on the evergreen- needled earth.

"You want to borrow my coat?" I reached out my down jacket to her.

"No, fine." She seemed a bit annoyed at my questions.

I wondered why she stayed here? Did she miss having company? She looked like she was more related to dirt than people. I just really wanted to know her name.

As I pulled out my sleeping bag, I noticed the crinkly notebook sitting in my pack. I'd forgotten I brought it up here. But if I found Sara, I wanted to show her I'd found it. Hoping that's what she wanted. It was a long drive if I had to take it back to New Mexico.

I snuggled in my sleeping bag while we laid in the silence, broken only by my gasp at the infrequent shooting stars.

I kept peering over at the woman, wondering if she was asleep. She didn't move or make any indications that she was uncomfortable. I was afraid she'd disappear if I shut my eyes. I fought hard to keep my eyelids up, but eventually gravity won.

***

The next morning, to my amazement, she was still there. Just sitting looking at the area where there was once a beautiful lush forest and people came from all over to see the wildflowers each August. The trees around us had blackened bark, but some grasses and wildflowers were peering out of the lightly burned soil.

The pain and sadness in her eyes betrayed her rigid stance.

"Good morning," I whispered, so as not to break the spell.

She nodded without a word.

I got out of the sleeping bag and rolled up my pad. I thoughtlessly took out the notebook so I could stuff my bag and pad back into my pack.

When I looked up, she was staring at the spiral bound book. It wasn't a look of recognition, but one more of disdain. *Did she think it bad form that I'd brought paper to the forest?*

I hesitated. Should I put it back or leave it out?

I left it out and sat down.

She stared at the tattered pages a little while longer and then looked back at the rising sun across the valley. I noticed the sun bouncing off her now glistening cheek.

Was she crying? She was as still as a statue.

I was still amazed she was here.

"I don't have much to offer you for breakfast- some nuts and water and one last granola bar, if you'd like," I whispered while pushing the granola bar her way.

She stood up and waved for me to follow.

I stared at her hand. I'd been waiting for this moment, for a connection to this woman, for her to say, "Who are you?" Instead she was beckoning me to follow, without words, without asking.

I wasn't sure I wanted to go.

Do I follow someone blindly into the woods?

I sat and stared, and she waited. No urging, no rushing, no impatience. Just standing there with quiet breaths, rooted to the earth.

I listened inward and asked myself, "*What do you want to do? Does going with her feel expansive or contracting?*" It felt good, it felt perfect, like everything was just on time.

I pushed myself off the ground, dusted myself off and walked toward Her. The woman I still didn't know. The notebook laid unopened on the dirt.

We walked up along a small stream, only a foot wide, the clear waters barely covered the rocky bed. She stopped and slurped the sparkling liquid from the cup of her hand.

She pointed at me, then at the stream. "Good water."

My chest tightened. I didn't have a filter or sterilizer with me, and here she was asking me to drink water straight from a stream. Water I had no idea from where it came. If I got sick out here, it would be bad. But something inside me said it was ok. I gently dipped my cupped left hand into the cool, clear waters. The waters sounded like a fish tank filter. A gentle hum exuded from the droplets, excited to see where they'd go and curving with the rocks and bank.

The trickle of cool water down my throat made my cells swell and swoon. It was more satisfying than anything I'd ever tasted. Even the 'spring' water I'd buy at the store was filled with unnatural flavors. My body could tell this was fresh from the earth. She was right, it was delicious.

I nodded my head and smiled at her, "Hmm, good."

She waved for me to follow again. We continued climbing alongside the creek, skirting wild rose bushes and willow trees, taking an ants meander up through the sparsely treed woods.

The sun was coming up and blazing down on my hatless head. When I packed, I hadn't really thought about the next day.

She suddenly stopped, pointed with her hand. "Eat.... Good...."

Was English not her primary language? I didn't detect an accent, but for some reason she didn't speak in sentences.

There, below her hand and to her right, were bright, shiny blackberries. My shoulders sunk. I was really hoping she was taking me to some exotic fruit that could only be found on this hillside. Not blackberries that can be bought in any grocery store here in the Northwest. But I was hungry, so I plucked one gently from the prickly branches, and popped it into my mouth. I have to say, I never was a big fan of store blackberries. They had a taste that wasn't quite complete. But this one berry had more flavor than 100 store-bought berries. It was like the difference between store-bought tomatoes and picking one right off the vine from your garden.

The juice spilled off my lips.

She laughed.

I pulled off more and shoved them into my mouth and let the juice spill over down my chin and neck. She did the same, laughing at herself, swirling and twirling and shaking the juice from her chin into the air. She played with the berries like a child. I followed suit.

Moments later, chipmunks, and golden mantled ground squirrels came out from under the bushes to see what the ruckus was about. They sat and watched, sniffing the air, but ready to crawl back into the bushes at a moment's notice.

She tapped her shoulder as if they should come sit on it, and I laughed some more.

But the joke was on me. I stood statue still as a chipmunk honored her request, crawled up the side of her skirt, across her right hand and arm and plopped down on her shoulder. I couldn't stop staring, but she didn't seem to notice. She handed a blackberry to her shoulder friend. He nibbled at it, little by little, chipping away at the black bumps and letting the juice drop onto her blouse. She kept dancing, more gently this time, and the chipmunk remained. Half of the berry plummeted to the ground and the earth-bound chipmunks made a dash for it. She giggled and offered him another. She looked at me, raised up her right arm and nodded for me to do the same. As if the chipmunk had done this trick before, he plopped the uneaten blackberry into his mouth and scampered down her arm and onto mine. I tried really hard not to laugh as his tiny claws tickled my bare skin. He ran right up my arm, into the nape of my neck and under my tiny ponytail. I just couldn't hold the laughter back! I was too ticklish. The chipmunk dug at my bunched hair as if he was going to make a nest. She laughed and laughed at the sight, continuing her juicy blackberry dance.

The chipmunk settled into the nape of my neck, and I gently moved my body, swaying to the sound of the ground's vibration.

She waved at me some more. "Come."

I pointed at the chipmunk and raised my eyebrows.

"Okay, come." She nodded.

"Okay, chipper, we're going for a bit of a ride," I whispered to my companion.

He didn't move or make a sound. I had the best new hair accessory. Instead of a barrette or rubber band, I'd been adorned with a chipmunk.

We followed along the side of the hill on the moist north-facing slope filled with spreading strawberries, and salmonberries. The air smelled of water droplets and honey. The woman and I made the only sounds, as a Cooper's Hawk flew over our heads hoping to wrestle up some birds for breakfast. This side of the hill doesn't get much sun, so the vegetation was much lusher and bushier than on the south-facing slopes, where only ponderosa or pinyon pines grow. The south-facing slopes are oven-ish, but much easier to walk on. This side required a lot of climbing over Mooseberry, White-flowered Rhododendron and around downed cedar; 500 yards felt like a mile.

We came up on a patch of bright red berries, tucked away under some Larch trees. *Wow, she was taking me on a visit to a wild smorgasbord this morning.* The berries were small, no bigger than the tip of my pinky finger, but like the blackberries, every cell burst with flavor and juice. I handed one to my hitchhiker, and I felt the blood red juice drip onto my skin.

When I offered the chipmunk another strawberry, his tiny dry snout touched my index finger as he grabbed it and stuffed it into his mouth. He ran down my back, jumped onto the ground and took off without even a thanks. The woman and I sat in silence, enjoying the crow caws for 10 minutes or so savoring the red goodness. Suddenly the woman, struck by a bolt of inspiration, jumped up and waved for me to follow her again.

More berries! I thought. I couldn't wait to see what she was going to show me next. *Maybe something I can't buy in a store!* It was definitely that. It was something you couldn't buy no matter how much money you had.

I tumbled back down the hill toward camp, while the woman practically floated through the brush. Some reason going down is harder for me, especially when having to tiptoe my way through thorny bushes and try not to stomp on wildflowers or berries. The gurgling waters gave us background music as the sun was brightening up the sky.

When we reached camp, the woman leaned over, picked up the notebook with her sunned, graceful hands and opened it in the middle. She stared a moment, smiled, and handed it back to me.

"Bring things." She glanced at me over her shoulder. I hesitated as she started walking toward the burned area. I shoved my things into my pack and threw it over my shoulder. She didn't seem interested in waiting for me.

I struggled to breathe as we crunched the scorched ground with our feet. Black statues stood all around. We moved through a colorless, lifeless planet. The hill, once filled with shade, was now a sauna of death. I wanted to go back to the green, but I trusted her guidance.

After about a mile, a force caused her to halt. She stood still and lowered her chin to her chest.

The experience overwhelmed me with sadness. I just wanted to sit down and comprehend the death created by a careless human. We can readily see the burned cars and timber, but we don't see the bones left by the animals who couldn't get out. We had passed by the skeleton of a black bear and her cub, a good mother not wanting to leave her child. There were other bones and fragments I couldn't readily identify as we trudged by. I could barely breathe. Breathing meant feeling the pinched nerve of sadness for a life carelessly lost.

All around us the ground was still black; the bodies of trees stood amongst the corpses of their cousins. The smaller trees, left after years of logging the old growth, couldn't withstand the hot, wind-fueled fires. They didn't have the girth for their bark to protect them from the intense flames. It left these hillsides full of char, with not one piece of green in sight. From what I'd learned in my Environmental Science studies, this told me this was a really burning fire. When I got my degree, I didn't really know what I'd do with it, but I loved being out here and being able to read the land.

Before people took hold, the bigger trees could handle ravaging fires started by lightning and provide seed for new trees and bushes and animals to come back. The human-caused fires created a topography that wasn't natural as they were often started during the driest of times. It would take decades for the trees to start growing again, if ever. In the meantime, we could only hope that enough vegetation returned to cover the soil before the fall rains caused it to all plow down to the creek beds. But often that didn't happen soon enough on its own.

I was startled from my grief when the woman took my hand, as if she heard my thoughts and understood my pain.

"Look." She pointed toward the ground.

"Yes, I see, ashes, coals, skeletons." The tears cleared paths through the dirt on my face.

"No, look, look deeper." She pointed. Her quiet voice was filled with a confident warmth.

I tilted my head to the side, trying to comprehend what she meant.

I looked at the black earth and stared some more. "I'm not sure what you want." I turned to her with pleading eyes, wanting to please her, to see what she saw.

She squatted down, still holding my hand and laid her right palm flat on the ground. "Beyond the surface, look for what you want to see." She nudged me to join her.

I joined her on the ground. "What I want to see is what WAS here," I choked. "The chipmunks running around, the strawberries and blackberries strewn about, the shade of the fir trees keeping the moisture in and the drying sun off."

'It's there, it's all there. You must see first, feel it here." She pointed to my chest. The only thing I felt was nausea. "Look." Her gentle voice had no judgment. She stared at the earth in front of her folded legs, laid the palms of her left hand gently on the ground next to her right hand and took a few deep breaths. I watched her silence as a smile brightened her eyes.

She stayed motionless for a few moments. Lost in her inner world. There were no sounds, not even a breeze, like nature was waiting with me to see what would happen. A subtle glow started emanating from her chest, down her arms and into her hands. The light penetrated the ground and disappeared into its depths.

I started to move my attention away, when a subtle movement caught my eye.

A brown-white roundness slowly wiggled itself up through the crusty earth. Gently, slowly, not sure of itself. The woman leisurely raised her hands as the umbrella shape continued to rise. Then out popped an edge and I saw a whole cap-the top of a mushroom! Shyly, the stealy brown stem pushed up and raised its cap inches above the ground, dirt falling off its smooth top. Next to the first mushroom, another started pushing through, and another-and another a foot from that!

I just stared, breathless, afraid it would all stop, and I'd wake up and discover it was all a dream.

She giggled at the sight, then turned to me and said, "Now you."

"Now me what?" I raised my eyebrows.

"See what's there." She pointed to the earth again.

"You mean those mushrooms are there under the ground here?"

She beamed and nodded.

"And you made them come up?" I stared.

She continued to nod.

"But how? I can't do that." I curled forward and shook my head.

"Yes, yes, you can. Just see. See them there." She beamed.

"That's all?" I was not convinced.

"Just relax, see them, feel them coming up. They are there," she crooned.

I squinted at the ground. "But why won't they come up by themselves then?"

"They will, but not soon enough."

"Soon enough for what?"

She ignored my question. "Just try. See them there." She nodded to the ground in front of my cramping, folded legs. It was more of a command than a request.

I took a deep breath and put my hands gently on the earth as she had, trying to imagine and feel the white tops of the mushrooms coming up. *But all I really saw was charred dirt.* I hung my head.

"Try again, it's okay." She gently took my hands and guided them back to the ground.

I took another deep breath. Tears flowed down my face. The sadness that I'd been holding in, the pain of seeing all this death, over-took my body and streamed down my face and watered the dark ground.

She just sat in silence, and placed her hands on top of mine.

It felt good. She touched me like my mother would. Gentle, kind, and understanding. I wanted to hug her. I didn't know I'd felt so alone. The world closed around us. We sat for a few minutes in silence until the tears dried up and I could breathe regularly again.

"It's ok. I understand. Come." She stood and was off again. I was overwhelmed. I didn't know if I could take anymore of this destruction. I wanted to run back to the green. I couldn't stand being amongst the corpses.

"Come, it's okay, you see." She turned back to me and waved her hand.

I wanted to believe her. I got up and followed in her footsteps for another mile across the barren land. Land that used to be filled with berries, and fir trees, scampering cottontails, and lumbering bears-all gone-all tortured by a careless fire. I stared at my shoes, trying not to take it in, wanting to run back the other way-but now there was no way I could find my way back. Sweat was pouring down my forehead, and I wished she'd take me to another stream.

She suddenly stopped and placed her hand on my shoulder. "Look"

As if she was reading my mind, I looked up and there was green! Bushes with bright red berries standing three feet high. Meadow rue and columbine showing their blue heads and in the midst was a little stream bubbling from the earth. She pointed. "Drink, it's good."

I felt guilty for taking any water from these plants, but I was parched. I bent down and lapped up the water from my cupped hand. The shallow streamed didn't even cover my palm.

I tiptoed away from the plants so as not to squash them, and just reveled in the green oasis in the midst of black.

She sat quietly behind me. I'd never seen water come straight from the earth. I'd never tasted how good it was. I was so engrossed in my thoughts and the miracle of seeing this life in a sea of death that I didn't even notice what she was doing. To her, it was the most natural thing. She didn't need photos or to show off. She didn't do it for anyone else but for the plants and animals themselves.

After 15 minutes or so, I took some more water from the earth's belly button and turned around toward her.

"That's so good," water dripping from my chin.

Then I saw what the ranger had described-a little oasis surrounding her. She was lost in thought, not even aware of my words.

Only moments ago, I'd crossed what was black and lifeless, and now she was sitting amidst grasses and seedlings!

I took a deep breath and just watched her. Her eyes were closed, her arms 90 degrees to her body, face turned up to the sky. I'd never seen anyone filled with so much peace.

As she sat there, more and more mushrooms sprouted around the edges of the oasis, then grasses and seedlings unfurled. Regrowth at hyper speed.

My brain's circuitry exploded and my body slumped. *How was this possible? How was she doing this?*

"Just see, just know it's all there," she whispered, reading my mind.

"I tried," I whined.

"Feel it, see it in your mind." She took a deep breath and released it slowly, like it was breathing life into the earth itself.

I laid back, exhausted at the thought of being able to do anything as extraordinary as this.

But I felt it anyway. I remembered how it felt when I first started connecting with Polly. How I had to expand my vision, and open my heart. So, I felt as if I were lying on lush grasses, and wildflowers popping up around me. I smelled the cleanness of green-filled air, the tinge of pine on my nostrils. I felt myself eating berries from the blackberry bushes and even heard a hummingbird buzzing over my head. The entire experience felt so good, felt so real, that I opened my eyes just to see.

She was staring at me, exposing her crooked teeth and the tip of her tongue. Not only did all the grass and plants feel real, it was! Only moments ago I'd laid down on blackness-and I woke up to green!

"Did you do that?" I asked.

"No, you." She pointed at me, as if to make sure I knew who she was talking about.

"No way!!"

She laughed, "Yes way! You saw it. It was there. You helped."

"So that's what you're doing here, helping this burn to regrow?" I said, looking out over the barren landscape.

"Not all." She pondered. "Just helping a bit. There's too much to do all by myself."

I felt giddy with delight.

I didn't know how it happened, but somehow I felt I'd contributed.

"Will it stay? Will it continue?" I ran my hands over the short, soft grass now surrounding my body.

"Yes, but we have to help it. Keep the dirt from going down the hill when it rains in a month or so."

"WE?" My eyebrows rose. *How did I suddenly become a part of this?*

"That's why you're here, to help," she assured me.

"Oh, okay." I might not believe it, but I didn't want to question her.

"You ask." She pointed at me.

I looked around. "Ask who?"

"You. You ask you. Do you want to stay and help?" She pointed to her chest.

I closed my eyes and took a deep breath. I posed the question silently. *Did I want to stay and help?*

My chest opened, and I felt light and tingly. *Yes, Yes, I absolutely did. All lights were green. I couldn't leave this.*

I still wondered, *Who IS this woman? Have I found Sara?*

Sara

I looked deeply in the eyes of my four-footed companion, "Clem, I need to leave you with our friends for a bit. I'll be back. You take good care of them, like you take of me." He licked my cheek for luck. I kissed him on the nose, then hugged each person who'd helped me know how good people can be.

I left Bessie hidden in some woods near Mt. Hood. It was the fire I felt I needed to take care of first. I threw on my pack out of habit. The roads were closed for miles around the fire, so I had to walk about 15 miles to get close. I didn't need to be in the midst of the fires, just in the vicinity.

My skin screamed for moisture. It was an unusually warm day. I found a creek bed and followed it up to get near the fire. I was challenged by the thickets of alder and huckleberry, and at the same time a path kept opening up to guide my way. The winds were blowing the smoke west, at least allowing my lungs to breathe clean air. With every bird call, and scat find, I became more and more determined to get to that fire and save all this innocent life. The animals were preparing for the winters, fattening up their stores; they didn't have time to be bullied by Brian and his rage.

I was lost in my determination and thirst after hiking until the afternoon.

"Hey! Whatcha' doing out here! It's not safe! Get out! NOW!" a soot covered man in a yellow coat yelled at me from up the hill.

I stopped in my tracks, startled by the sudden company. I closed my eyes, took a deep breath and felt the courage in my belly. "I'm here to help! I can get this out for you." Everything seemed so unusually loud with all the chain saws, the crackling of trees and the roar of the fire a mile away. How had I not heard this before?

"Lady, WE can't get this out and I've been doing this a long time. Get out NOW!" He put down his chainsaw and pointed back the way I'd come. He took his walkie-talkie out of his jacket and started speaking into it, keeping an eye on me. "Charlie, some nut job is out here thinking she can take out the fire. Send someone to get her. I don't have time for this."

While he was distracted in conversation, I took off running, dodging around him and towards the fire. He was cutting a safety line, and I needed to be closer. After I was well out of his sight and could feel the heat of the flames, an invisible arm blocked my path. I bent over, gasping for air. When I could finally stand up-right I thought, "This is it." Every cell in my body said, "Start here."

Start what? I still had no idea. This was much bigger than the little fire I had put out on the farm. Even after all I'd seen, I couldn't believe this little creek was going to help much.

"Hey, Lady! Stop! Get the hell out of here! Are you crazy?' Another yellowed jacketed man came out of the cover of slender fir trees.

"YESSSS!" I screamed back with my whole body. It stopped him mid stride.

"Leave me alone, I can do this!" I stood my ground, arms outstretched, as if creating an invisible shield around me.

"Not on my watch, you ain't." He started running toward me.

I took off the other way, zigging and zagging over the cut logs, and creeping snowberry. He was carrying a lot more weight. "We're wasting time. Leave me alone, I'm not your responsibility!" I shouted over my shoulder.

"Looks like you are today." He said cockily, like he thought he was really going to catch up to me.

After about 2 minutes of running on the bumpy terrain, he panted, "Come on, Lady, I got better things to do than chase you!" His lungs gulped for air as the words came out of his mouth.

"Me too!" I shouted back, not slowing down a bit. "Leave me alone! Let me do my work, you'll see. I'm not a martyr...."

He stopped, so I halted and turned towards him. "We're wasting time. I'm not gonna throw myself into the fire!"

He leaned and put his hands just above his knees, still trying to catch his breath. "Okay, I gotta get back to work. Just don't get yourself killed." He took a deep breath and walked back the way we'd come with his chainsaw over his shoulder. I was impressed that he'd been running with that thing.

"Thanks! I won't!" I waved at him as if he'd just given me a hitch somewhere.

The fire jumper headed back towards his crew and left me to myself. It was the first time I'd noticed it. *It was HOT!!!* Like a pizza oven. There wasn't any movement but the flowing smoke.

It was odd. I'd expected to see animals running from the flames, but either they were long gone or were staying away from people. My belly tightened realizing the wild blaze could turn toward me at any minute. The smells and sounds kept changing, depending on what was lit up. It was like a war zone, explosions erupted all around, and I didn't know where the next blow would come from. The damp charcoal took on a flavor that my lungs didn't want to take in. It was eerie. I didn't know what to do, but I knew I had to do it quickly.

My body trembled with helplessness. I felt overpowered by the devastation of the erupting force. My nostrils struggled to find something my lungs could use as the thick ash particles of a tree's death choked my lungs. Many people think cutting down more trees is the answer. Funny how getting rid of something seems to always be the answer rather than being responsible people. The most devastating fires are almost always caused by human carelessness, or worse, like this one, caused by a cry for attention.

I looked at the towering Douglas fir and the small spruce trees around me. I put my arms above my head and loudly whispered, "Trees help me! I don't know what to do!"

Nothing.

" Come on, how are you quiet NOW?" When I get scared or angry, it's not pretty.

"Fuck it!" I yelled and ran back to the creek.

I knelt at the water's edge as it flowed down the hill. I was at the altar, praying. "Okay, creek, I need you to direct all your water to the fire now." I was stammering, full of fear it wouldn't work. That I'd come all this way for nothing.

Nothing changed.

What the hell is going on? I wondered.

I stood and looked at the fire a mile or so away, trying to contain my shivers. Then I remembered something I'd seen over and over again. If a peaceful spot got crowded, I often found an even better camping place. If I wanted to make a left turn but couldn't, going straight took me to where I really wanted to be but had forgotten.

If something wasn't working, I was headed the wrong way. I was being guided a different way. I nodded. "Okay, what is the easiest path in front of me? Go somewhere else?" I talked out loud, hoping the trees would chime in.

My chest tightened. "No..." I continued, "the water source?" I felt a release in my belly and chest. " Yes, I need more water." I whispered.

"Of course! How do I get that?" And there it was. When I asked the question, the answer appeared. High above me amid the crackling and fire roar, came the chomp, chomp, chomp of helicopter blades cutting the air far above me.

"The helicopters," the trees murmured.

"What? Are you crazy? I can't fly a helicopter!" I looked up through the tree boughs.

Then I saw it.

"Oh crap! What have I gotten myself into?" I shook inside, I didn't know how I was gonna get up there.

"Okay guys, I really need some help here." I turned in a circle, hoping an eagle would come, or the trees would grow some lower branches I could climb.

Then I heard Joel's voice just as if he was standing right next to me.

"We all can fly."

I covered my ears with my hands. "What?! No, no, no, you don't understand. I'm afraid, I mean I'm deathly afraid of heights. Have you noticed I've never even CLIMBED a tree?"

Nothing.

"CRAP, CRAP, CRAP!! I don't want to do this!!" They didn't ask me.

As I was shaking my head and pushing my hands against my ears even tighter, I began feeling air under my feet and the ground started falling from underneath me. Slowly, inch by horrid inch I got further and further from my beloved earth. "No! No.... wait, please wait.... There has to be a better way." My body shuddered fearful tears. My feet dangled above the bushes and kept rising until they were at the level of the lowest branches of the surrounding trees.I didn't know what to do, it was just happening. I could barely breathe.

"Ohhhhh, I don't like this! They're really gonna think I'm a witch now!" I reached out my hands, trying to grab onto something. I think I heard the trees LAUGHING!

"You laughing at me?" I smiled to the air. "Well, just wait until you're charred for thinking I could freakin' fly!"

"Just don't look down," they offered.

Which, of course, caused me to look down. *Bad idea, really bad idea.* I was halfway up the side of a mature hemlock. That meant I was HIGH! I wanted to focus on parts of these beauties I'd never seen up close, but I was freakin' flying! I was just trying to catch my breath.

"Now what?" I kicked my legs and tried to touch the hemlock.

Nothing. They knew I already knew and I was just hoping the plan had changed.

"Crapppp!" I shook my head, and took a deep breath. I relaxed a bit as my body continued to float up to the tops of the trees. I felt their confidence in me as they lifted me up above their heads, assuring me they'd catch me if I fell. I heard the trees struggling to breathe through the ash-filled air and as I cleared the treetops I saw the flames leaping out of the forest nearby. I realized then, I didn't have time to be scared. There was no room for pity. Lives were at stake. The well-being of my best friends, the ones who'd been my constant companions, and loved me when no one else did. I could return the favor, and the time was now. Courage bubbled within my belly and seeped up my spine and into my frizzled mind. Clarity washed over me and instead of focusing on what scared me, I focused on what I wanted to accomplish.

I looked down at the creek, as she looked at me, waiting for guidance. I took a gulp of air. "Okay creek, come with me," I commanded as I waved my arms. And as if it were the most natural thing in the world, the creek in all its crystal, tingly, glory started flowing UP!

The water kept coming down the hillside, and when the path started going up, all the water behind it did too. I'd seen it in Ilanaly before, but that it did it upon my command, on earth, was bewildering, but there was no time for questions.

The water collected in an ever-expanding pool near my waist. *What was gonna happen to all that water when it got to be too much?* I didn't know, and I sure didn't want to find out.

I don't know how I was doing it, it didn't feel like me at all. I flew above the treetops and the creek just followed me, like a puppy following its mom.

"This is crazy!" I shouted down to the treetops. "They're gonna kill me!" The blades of the helicopter were getting closer and closer, and I still didn't know how it was going to help.

"You'll know what to do," the trees murmured.

"Yeah, you keep saying that."

Whomp, whomp, whomp.... The blades of the helicopter were slashing through the air, closer and closer. Suddenly, it was only feet from my head.

About peeing in my pants. I shouted, "go down!"

And down I went-still above the treetops, but low enough I dragged my toes. "Sorry guys!"

They giggled like I was tickling them.

The helicopter was headed toward the near edge of the fire. I didn't know how to fly. I didn't have an accelerator, but I remembered all the episodes of Superman my brothers made me sit through. So I put my arms out like Superman, trying to gain some speed. *Crazy. But it worked!*

As I got close behind the helicopter I saw what I was looking for. The helicopter had a big bucket of water hanging far below its belly. I knew I needed to get to them before they dumped that bucket.

The creek, like a tether to some distant root, just kept following.

If anyone sees this, they're gonna lock me up.

But the firefighters on the ground were too busy trying to stop the rampaging fire, and the helicopter pilot was too busy trying to hit his target.

I got to the swinging bucket. I was sure it had a fancier name, and grabbed the upper edge. Thank goodness I hadn't eaten much in the last two weeks.

I waved to the creek waiting for direction. "HERE!! Go in here! Just keep filling this. They'll know what to do."

I think the water knew where to go, but like life in the forest, working together, working with each other, giving and receiving, always leads to greater things, the water was used to being a part of the whole. The water particles were used to having the fungi and roots direct it to where it would help the plants the most. That's what the quenching waters were doing with the firefighters now, letting them show her where they needed her the most, even if the firefighters didn't know it.

As I hung 100 feet in the air, mesmerized at the flowing water, another miracle began leaping up from the forest floor. Not only did the creek that had been tethered to me by some invisible force pour itself into the bucket like a spigot into a pond, but ALL the creeks in the area rose up out through the trees, like glitter pouring from its container. They waterfalled all over the area where the helicopter poured its water.

That got the firefighters attention. They stood looking up, with open mouths.

I was laughing so hard, I added to the help with my own water trickling out through my pant legs.

The waters just kept coming. They took over, just pouring into the flames, so I climbed up the rope to the helicopter. I figured I had some explaining to do.

The cabin doors were off, so I grabbed the edge of the helicopter just behind the co-pilot's seat. I was high on adrenaline and gratitude.

"Hi, fellas!" I waved once I'd crawled inside.

The pilot looked back and furrowed his brows. "How.. how...did you get in here?" He quickly turned back toward the front. "JJ," he said to the co-pilot, "deal with that."

I ignored them. "Hey, I need you to stay here. Those creeks will take care of things. They just need some guidance on the best places to go."

The pilot looked at the co-pilot. "JJ, am I awake? What the hell is happening?"

I laughed, understanding their confusion. "You're awake, I can't explain any of this now." As if I was going to be able to explain it later. "Please, just go where you need the creeks to go and they'll follow. I've got to get to the other side!" I screamed through the noise of the open chopper.

The pilot glanced back at me, "Lady, this is dangerous territory. If you're not a figment of my imagination, then you better just sit down, and buckle up."

He was on a mission, but so was I. "I hear you, but I'm going."

The co-pilot peered around his seat at me. "No! No! you can't do that! It's too dangerous over there. The wind is moving things that way. We're not even flying over there." He turned back around, thinking that was the end of the conversation. *It definitely wasn't.*

I patted him on the shoulder. "I'll think of something." I hesitated for a moment, realizing I was going to leave familiar territory again, like a parachutist without a parachute. I was putting myself back into the hands of the forest and trees and the natural forces I'd unleashed.

I took a deep breath, released my grip, and jumped from the helicopter. The air below the helicopter scooped me up and flung me on my way.

"STOOOPPP!" I heard shouting behind me. I giggled.

Fuck! I can't believe I'm going to the leading edge of this thing. I'm crazy! I laughed to myself, thinking of all the people who'd said that to me in the past. Had my accepting my unusualness, truly unleashed my abilities because I was no longer holding myself back?

The creeks in the area stayed with the helicopter. I gained some elevation so as not to get stung by the flames, and headed to the front edge of the fire. It was headed toward a grove of Sequoias that I used to sleep among. Somehow, they'd never come under the loggers' ax. There was this little nook of them, as if the loggers too were overtaken by their beauty and wanted their kids to see it too. As I flew toward them I remembered camping there several years earlier. It was one of the most special places I'd been. The sun filtered through those towering candles, feeling like a peace filled dusk even in the middle of the day. The air was filled with nourishing droplets. It was a fairy land, and I was a spec among these gentle giants. The decaying material gathered around the Sequoia's and the ground squished beneath my feet. The air hummed perfection and serenity. Their energy created its own atmosphere and a hush I'd never experienced anywhere else.

The crackling flames brought me back, fearing the worst for the Micah Grove. What would happen if the creeks were dried up? *What am I gonna do if even the helicopters won't fly over there?* I was a twine of knowing and doubt.

I arrived at the edge of the grove. Smoke filled every gap. I was flying blind, but somehow with sight.

"Don't worry, the creeks will just cover it," I heard a Sequoia say as I stared at the dry ground.

And there, 500 yards in front of me, out of the fire-raging canopy, came all the creeks in the area flowing up to the top and above the flames, over to the trees just in front of the flames. I didn't have to do anything. A door had been opened, and the forest got to work saving itself. I even started seeing birds flying over and pooping on the fire to help. "This is our home, too." said a Raven.

The firefighters uphill of the ascending fire didn't even notice what was happening. Those human heroes of the wild world were working as hard as they could to cut a path the fire couldn't jump.

My method helped more animals from losing their homes.

I really don't know where all the water came from. It was like it just started pouring out of the earth-like a valve opened on the ground and all the underground streams started flowing towards the fire.

The grove was saved, the flames died back. And the resulting smoke filled in the valleys. But there was still a lot of work to do.

Maxine

We spent the day walking to various spots in the burned area. It was a 500,000 acre burn. It would take most people two days to walk across it. One of the biggest wildfires in Oregon history. All because people decided to not to put their hands on the campfire coals and make sure it was really out.

My guide, whose name I still didn't know, seemed to know where the water seeped from the ground. So we'd start there. We went back to a couple of the places she'd already started, to make sure they were okay, or see what they needed. When the sun lowered behind a distant hill, we returned to where we slept the night before. This woman carried nothing with her and I'd only brought enough food for one day. *What were we going to eat?*

"Want me to go get food from my car?" I asked.

"Just wait," she put her hand out and nodded.

We'd been out hiking all day up and down hills and steep terrain, some best suited for mountain goats. I'd been fine all day drinking from the springs, but now the lack of food had caught up with me. I really didn't want to hike down to the car and back. That was another four miles and mostly in the dark.

But what was she waiting for? Was she going to grab a bat out of the air and eat that?

"Can we go get more of those blackberries?" I proposed.

She turned toward me, smiled, and squeezed my right hand.

"Something better," she murmured.

She didn't have a gun. I hadn't seen any signs of animals since the chipmunks. Surely we weren't going to eat our friends!

"No chipmunks. Better." She laughed.

I shook my head. She really was reading my mind! I wanted to tell her to stop it. It felt rude, but it was nice not to have to speak. Speaking out here felt like speaking in church while someone was saying a prayer or the choir was singing. I preferred hearing the earth's hum, like a parent singing a lullaby. "Rest" hummed the earth, "It's all right, you're safe." No condemnation, no telling you what you have to do-just quiet praise.

From our overlook, I sprawled back on my elbows, watching the sun's bright yellow turn to soft oranges and reds. I recalled my journey here. My thoughts were different. I felt less anxious and happier than I'd ever been. More content than I even thought possible. But thoughts of steak, salmon, and chocolate chip cookies kept creeping in. *Any and all of it sounded so good.*

The sun finally went to visit the other side of the earth, and the stars became the center of the show.

I hoisted myself up and walked to my pack. My legs ached. If I couldn't get food, I could at least sleep. I pulled out my sleeping pad and bag, spread them out a few feet from my friend, and crawled inside. I was elbow-deep into my bag when I heard the familiar voice again. The voice that I longed to hear at one point, but had mostly forgotten by now. The voice I'd spent an entire night listening to. The voice that just disappeared, that I looked for for days-and there it was again, only a few feet away.

"Hey, Grandma! Teaching ole' Maxine here your things?!"
I looked up toward the voice, baffled by her presence. She
looked just the same, her voice still familiar. I wanted to be
mad, I wanted to scream, but I was just so happy to see her
again.

"Molly?" I said, barely audible. "Wha, Wha, how did you get
here? Did I hear you say Grandma?" I slipped out of my bag,
never taking my eyes off her.

"Hi, Max! I knew you'd find your way here if I left you
alone." She threw her pack on the ground and knelt next to the
woman I'd been following all day. They hugged and greeted
each other.

I was on the verge of tears. "Wait, what? You intentionally
left?" I felt like someone had punched me in the stomach. I
trusted this woman with all my secrets, things I'd not said to
anyone. I thought she'd always be there, that we'd never lose
touch after that night, but she just left, abandoned me, without
a word.

*And now she just shows up and pretends everything is the
same?* I wanted to run, I wanted to scream. I wanted to go
home.

"Oh, Maxie, that's such a long story, and I know you're
starving. Come on over here. I've got food!" She patted the
ground next to her.

I was definitely starving, but my hurt and curiosity were
stronger.

"Come sit down. I brought a feast!" She opened the top of
her pack to show me the delights.

Molly opened her backpack, spread out a blanket and started filling it with crackers, cold cuts, raw veggies and chocolate! My favorite chocolate even!

The woman and Molly distributed everything in complete
silence. Molly patted the blanket. "Come join us. I'll answer
questions later, okay?"

My stomach pulled me forward. I sat on the edge of the brightly covered blanket. We gave thanks for the day and food, and dug in. No talking, just savoring each bite. There's something about eating on the ground and in the woods, with silence and stars as the background, that just makes everything taste better. Each bite burst with flavor and my cells rushed to take in its nutrients and repair the days' damage. Even though I was starving, I couldn't just shove the food in my mouth, like I'd do at work. That felt sacrilegious and ungrateful. It was like I was eating the earth itself and I had to care for each bite that I'd been graciously given. The darkness made it difficult for us to see the food, and like walking in the dark, each chew was measured and studied. As angry as I was, I also felt like I was with family. People I'd known all my life, and yet saw me more than ever before. No words were necessary, we could just enjoy the calm.

After my belly was filled and the chocolate was melting in my mouth. I laid flat on the ground and sighed. My mind was blank. All the hurt had dissolved.

"You staying the night?" I asked Molly.

"Yep, no big fires right now, so I'll stay a few days and help." Her voice carried through the blackness. The questions came back, but the need for sleep was overwhelming.

I crawled back into my sleeping bag and allowed the blanket of stars to fall over me. The woman and Molly shared the blanket, shoulder to shoulder.

The questions swirled in my head, as my body closed shop for the night. *Who were these people? Grandma? Could Sara have a grandchild? There was no talk of her having a baby in the notebook. Was this Sara at all?*

***

The next morning I sat and stared at the two women, waiting for them to wake up. I didn't know the time, but the first rays of light were tapping the hill tops to the east.

I was feeling played. Like these two women had somehow dragged me along on some secret mission of theirs-and I was just a puppet at the end of their strings. I was ready to pack up and leave, but the questions kept me still. I'd hear their answers and then take off. I didn't need to be a part of anyone's games.

If only it had been that simple.

"Good morning, Max." Molly sang out as she stretched her arms and sat up.

"Hi," I responded sternly.

"I'm sorry if you feel jilted. I'll get to your questions. Be right back." Molly disappeared into the woods. The older woman smiled at me, got up and headed a different way.

Would they come back? At least I had some food.

***

I visited the woods, packed my sleeping bag and pad, and took out the notebook. I felt done with it. I wanted to give it back. It'd led me on a wild goose chase, into things I wasn't even sure were real. *Was this really just a long dream?*

A few minutes later, they both came back and sat down on their bright cover. Molly patted the blanket and called me over. "Bring the notebook."

I got up and handed it to her. "I was about to give it back," I gruffly responded.

Molly shrugged her shoulders. "Your choice."

I sat down next to Molly, with the other woman on her far side. The sun's rays were lifting behind us, warming our backs, and the ice was melting from my bones.

Molly pointed to the woman I'd been hanging out with. "This is Lilly, Sara's Mom."

She put her hand to her chest. "I'm Sara and Joel's daughter." The woman I now knew as Lilly just stared out into space. "During the season, I work with the fire crews, helping them put out fires. Started years ago." She looked out into space, remembering. "I work nights so the press doesn't see me. None of us want the publicity." She looked into my eyes to see if she could trust me with her secrets.

"Sometimes Mom, who you know as Sara, and I work together. In the summer there's so many fires we usually work apart. People don't even realize the number of fires we put out." She shook her head, eyes filled with sadness.

I sat motionless, tense, staring at Molly. The birds were singing their morning praises, and the freshness of a new day filled my nostrils.

She continued, "We saw a vision that someone from the outside would join us. When you told me you were looking for Sara, I went to find Mom and let her know."

My shoulders relaxed, and my chest opened. I took a big breath and let it out with a sigh. *Oh, that makes sense.* "Why didn't you just tell me?"

Molly laid her hand on mine. "It had to be your choice, your desire. You had to want to be here. Make sense?" Her face was full of compassion and kindness.

I sat and breathed in the dewy air, remembering how I got here and feeling like a willing puppet. A marionette that had been protected from herself and led on a lifelong adventure that I would have never found myself. Things made sense. The pieces of the vast puzzle had come together more beautifully than I could ever have thought. That's the way it always works, when we let it.

There was still a key piece missing.

Sara

As I flew (it still feels weird to write that. I flew without an engine. I understand if you don't believe me. I wouldn't.)

The air rushed through my hair and across my skin. I was still bewildered by being above the treetops. It was a view I'd always wanted to experience. I thought I'd be in a plane. The awareness that I couldn't count on helicopter support over here, didn't bother me. It was like I was being guided incrementally to what was really possible. *Shouldn't the water know to go onto the flames?* How was I to know what water knew?

Could I make it rain? Popped into my head. *Oh! What a great idea.* I was feeling more confident. There was a force much greater than me at work here. I was just the conduit. All I had to do was believe and it would be done. *If I could make it rain, really pour down like a good winter storm, then that would really take the fires out.* I couldn't do that from the air. I needed a quiet place. I shook my head and giggled. *Here I was contemplating things like I was sitting under a tree, not 100 feet above them.*

I saw a remote hilltop that provided the perfect vantage point. I zoomed over to the hilltop, until.....

I realized I had to land.

Shit! How am I gonna do that? It's all trees!

I didn't have time to figure it out. The fire raged on. So I looked for the least bit of clearing in these brushy woods and just visioned myself landing gently on the ground, feet first.

Okay, well, it didn't go like that at all, but I survived.

After getting my wits back from a bumpy arrival, I sat up on the dry, rocky ground and looked up to the sky. The blue was surrounded by dark grey billowy clouds careening from the forest below. "Sky," I said gently, "the forest needs your help, it needs some rain."

A northern pygmy owl tooted in the distance.

I really had to improve on my requests. Nature seemed to be unimpressed.

So, covered in soot and smoke, I sat looking towards the flames, and just visualized it pouring down rain over the entire fire. I could feel the quiet, the petrichor of rain, and dampened smoke. I saw all the trees still green, and the ground covered in thimbleberries. I felt joy rushing through my veins as the fire was being doused in the downpour of rain. I could hear the firefighters whooping it up in celebration, and the trees thankfulness. All this I saw in my mind and experienced in my body.

I was in a bubble of quiet, even the birds were visualizing with me.

I don't know how long I sat there, doing that, I just waited for that smell of wetness I love.

And I waited.

And waited, and waited.

All the stillness welled up inside of me and exploded through my mouth.

"Please! I need some help here!" I screamed at the sky. "The plants and animals need your help! Where are you now? Where the fuck are you when we need you?"

I punched at the air, throwing fingers towards the sky, and screamed until my throat was sore. I laid down on the ground, sobbing at feeling so helpless, so unheard.

I must have fallen asleep.

I awoke as the sun was starting her journey towards the horizon. It looked about 5 pm, but what I felt startled me. The feeling I longed for, the soft kisses of the earth, the smell of rejuvenation.

Rain, the gentle drops of life.

I looked towards the blaze. There above it were huge dark blue Nimbostratus clouds, pouring down in swaths of moisture, like a waterfall, onto the fire.

The planes weren't flying; the roar had quieted, and I could no longer see the flames leaping from the tops of trees.

"Thank you," I whispered, "thank you." I bowed my head. I was humbled. All the adrenaline poured out of my body, leaving me a lifeless lump.

I laid there, letting the rain charge my pores, every inch of my clothing moist. Frozen with gratitude. The shower filled me with awe and appreciation for the earth, for all this being taken care of while I slept. It just needed me to let go, let them do the work.

And they did.

***

I made my way back to the firefighting base that night, keeping my feet on the earth.

No one questioned who I was. I guess I fit in, all covered in soot, dirt and wild hair.

The crews were celebrating with beers and stories. I wanted to tell someone, I wanted to share the moment with someone, but, who was going to believe me?

I joined a campfire ring full of guys who looked like they just walked off the fire line. They were fighting off fatigue with a lot of laughter.

I sat in anonymity for a while, savoring the comradery with people all fighting for a similar cause. It didn't last.

"Hey! You're that woman who showed up in my helicopter!" I looked around, and there, staring at me, was the helicopter pilot who I had directed the streams to follow.

I wanted to run, but I also wanted to know what had happened was real.

One guy nudged him. "Don't worry about Jerry. He must've inhaled too much smoke."

"No, you guys saw it!" he yelled, pointing at me. "You guys saw those streams pouring down over the flames and filling my bucket. Tell 'em what you did." He glared in my direction.

I just stared back, pleading with him to not tell, and yet wanting to talk with him.

"Jerry, give her a break." One guy poked his leg. "She's exhausted, like the rest of us."

"Well, she should be. She was fuckin' flying!" He spread out his arms like wings, a beer in one hand. "She jumped right out of my helicopter, almost spilled my whole bucket!"

"Jerry, go to bed." said another tired voice from around the fire. "You're so full of shit."

"What's your name?" Another guy asked.

I couldn't answer.

"Hey, I know you!" Another yellow-jacketed man stood up. " You're the woman I had to chase all over when you crossed the fire line." He mimicked chasing arms pumping. "You're more nuts than Jerry. Glad to see you made it out." He lifted his beer to me.

"Yeah, she made it out 'cause she was flying with creeks following her. That was some crazy shit. JJ, tell 'em." Jerry chimed in again.

I was starting to regret coming here. I was at a crossroads. Did I go left or right? My body made her choice. Slowly, steadily, she opened up. A zipper started in my calves and worked itself up to my neck. Everything I'd been hiding since I was a kid flew out, light shone in the dark. I no longer felt ashamed of myself and how different I was. I'd done a great thing today. If it wasn't for me, those guys would still be out there in 200 degree heat and more plants and animals would lose their homes.

The zipper continued up my throat and out of my mouth. "It was me," I said casually, as if I were saying my name.

Jerry jumped back up. "See, told you guys I wasn't makin' that shit up."

"What? You were flying?" the guy next to Jerry asked. "You got water to follow you?"

"Yeah, and I made it rain." I beamed.

Twenty pairs of eyes just looked at me as if my head had popped off, beer cans motionless.

Maxine

After the talk with Molly, I went out to the burned area by myself. I needed the time to thank the forces for guiding me here, to feel what was next. I laid on the earth, drawing in her wisdom and strength. *Am I supposed to be here with these people? What do I want to do now?*

My body felt like an electrical cord without a ground. I didn't feel I was doing much, yet mushrooms and grasses kept popping up in the areas I sat. I squealed in delight at each new life. It never felt like they were coming up because of me. Rather they were coming up for me, as a gift, for seeing that they were there all along.

I was dreaming of rain and an oasis, asleep in a patch of grass that'd sprung up around me. The hot piercing sun made it hard to stay awake, without the shade of the evergreens that used to thrive here.

"Hi, Max," said a voice. I woke up from my nap, still in that foggy place where reality and sleep intermingle and you're not sure if you're dreaming.

I covered my eyes from the blinding sun. Above me stood a shadow of a figure with the sunlight pouring around her edges.

Her voice sounded just like I'd expected it to sound. Mothering with a bit of roughness. Deep and soothing, like it was made of soil. Her long, sun-bleached hair pulled back in a ponytail. Her eyes clear blue like a high mountain lake.

She sat down beside me as I sat up. She didn't have to say who she was. I knew. There was no mistaking it this time.

'Sara?"

She smiled and nodded.

I beamed. I'd found her. *Well, I guess she found me.*

"You've done some beautiful work here." She looked around at the green. "Thank you for all you're doing to bring back the plants. We really appreciate it." She had the gentlest face, flowing with love as she looked into my eyes.

"Your journal... your story.... I had to find you. I didn't know why, I just did," I stammered.

"I'm glad you did." She put her hand on mine.

It was the start of a new day.

About the Author

HJ Corning can be found dancing in the woods eating Montezuma's 100% chocolate and drinking Zevia.

Then The Trees Said Hello is her debut novel. It is the first in the Ilanaly series.

It sprouts from a life lived in the woods, hiking, backpacking and just sitting under trees far from civilization.

She lives in the mountain southwest with her engineer husband, ball chasing dog and lap loving cat.

Go to www.hjcorning.com, to receive occassional emails about my new books and deals, get your free prequel to the Ilanaly series and sign up here.

Acknowledgments

Thank you for the incredibly supportive Smucker's NMN novel group. Thank you to my early readers, Kim, Belinda, Ron and Linda. Thank you to Caroline, for polishing the story. And thank you to Jim, for never shutting the door, so I was free to fly!

Made in the USA
Middletown, DE
22 October 2023